W9-CTI-924

A NEWBERY ZOO

A NEWBERY ZOO

A dozen
animal stories
by Newbery Award—winning
authors

Selected by
Martin H. Greenberg
and
Charles G. Waugh

Introduction by Betsy Byars

DELACORTE PRESS/NEW YORK

Published by Delacorte Press
Bantam Doubleday Dell Publishing Group, Inc.
1540 Broadway   New York, New York 10036

Acknowledgments

"Mr. Wilmer's Strange Saturday," copyright 1945 by Robert Lawson, renewed 1972 by Nina Forbes Bowman. Reprinted by permission of the estate of Nina Forbes Bowman.

"He Lion, Bruh Bear, and Bruh Rabbit," from *The People Who Could Fly*, by Virginia Hamilton, illustrated by Leo and Diane Dillon. Text copyright 1985 by Virginia Hamilton. Illustrations copyright 1985 by Leo and Diane Dillon. Reprinted by permission of Alfred A. Knopf, Inc.

"The Dancing Camel," copyright 1965 by Betsy Byars. Reprinted by permission of the author.

"The Wounded Wolf," copyright 1978 by Jean Craighead George. Reprinted by permission of Curtis Brown, Ltd.

"Bess and Croc," from *Bess and the Sphinx*, copyright 1948, 1967 by Elizabeth Coatsworth. Reprinted by permission of Kate Barnes.

"Tom and Jerry," from the *Will James Book of Cowboy Stories*, copyright 1935 by Will James. Reprinted by permission of Will James Art Company, 2237 Rosewyn Lane, Billings, MT 59102.

"Henry and Ribsy Go Fishing," from *Henry and Ribsy*, copyright 1954 by Beverly Cleary. Reprinted by permission of Morrow Junior Books, a division of William Morrow and Co., Inc.

"The Cat and the Golden Egg," from *The Town Cats and Other Tales*, by Lloyd Alexander. Copyright 1979 by Lloyd Alexander. Used by permission of Dutton Children's Books, a division of Penguin Books USA Inc.

"Fireflies," from *Joyful Noise*, copyright 1988 by Paul Fleischman. Reprinted by permission of HarperCollins Publishers.

"The Black Fox," "Discovery at the Field," "The Forest Chase," and "Hazeline," from *The Midnight Fox*, by Betsy Byars. Copyright 1968 by Betsy Byars. Used by permission of Viking Penguin, a division of Penguin Books USA Inc.

"The Rascal Crow," from *The Foundling and Other Tales of Prydain*, by Lloyd Alexander. Copyright 1973 by Lloyd Alexander. Reprinted by permission of Henry Holt and Company, Inc.

Library of Congress Cataloging-in-Publication Data

A Newbery zoo: a dozen animal stories by Newbery award–winning authors / selected by Martin H. Greenberg and Charles G. Waugh; introduction by Betsy Byars.
    p. cm.
    Contents: The rascal crow / Lloyd Alexander—Henry and Ribsy go fishing / Beverly Cleary—He Lion, Bruh Bear, and Bruh Rabbit / Virginia Hamilton—Tom and Jerry / Will James—Fireflies / Paul Fleischman—Mr. Wilmer's strange Saturday / Robert Lawson—The wounded wolf / Jean Craighead George—Bess and Croc / Elizabeth Coatsworth—The black fox / Betsy Byars—A tale of the poplar / Charles Boardman Hawes—The cat and the golden egg / Lloyd Alexander—The dancing camel / Betsy Byars.
    ISBN 0-385-32263-1
    1. Children's stories, American. [1. Animals—Fiction. 2. Short stories.] I. Greenberg, Martin Harry. II. Waugh, Charles.
PZ5.N397   1995
[Fic]—dc20
                                          94-32712
                                            CIP
                                            AC

Manufactured in the United States of America

April 1995

10 9 8 7 6 5 4 3 2 1

MPV

TABLE OF CONTENTS

Contents

Betsy Byars

INTRODUCTION

EVERY SATURDAY, AS a child, I went to the movies. There were always, in addition to the main attraction, a cartoon, a newsreel and a serial. If I was lucky, the serial starred Clyde Beatty.

Clyde Beatty was an animal trainer. He knew more about animals than anybody in the world. I wanted to be just like him when I grew up—not so much for the glory of the circus ring or the excitement of the jungle captures (although I certainly would have participated fearlessly and wholeheartedly in both). What I longed for was an entrance into the magical world of animals.

I read a lot of animal books and stories, too. They let me enjoy vicarious thrills I couldn't have any other way. The stories had everything—pathos, adventure, excitement, suspense and humor, the same mixture you will find in this collection.

There is a wide variety of stories here. Some are make-believe. The animals talk. This is fun because the animals surprise us with their insight and intelligence, whether it's Virginia Hamilton's plain speaking Bruh Rabbit, Lloyd Alexander's Quickset, the clever cat companion who sharpens knives and cooks, or Kadwyr, his nimble, teasing crow. In stories like these, I get the feeling that what these creatures say is what they really would say if given the chance.

Some of the authors mix make-believe into the real world. Elizabeth Coatsworth gives us two delightfully believable children who share a dreadful secret acquaintance with a make-believe crocodile. Robert Lawson muses on what would happen if an average insurance clerk discovered he could speak "animal." And in "The Dancing Camel," the desert is real but the camel isn't.

Other authors tell of extraordinary encounters with real-life animals. In "The Black Fox," Tom and I (and you) follow a fox together. Will James tells of a remarkable friendship between two horses. Jean Craighead

George tells the story of "The Wounded Wolf" as if she were able to observe everything the wolf feels and does with scientific accuracy.

And there's more—excitement and adventure in Charles Boardman Hawes's "The Tale of the Poplar," poetry in Paul Fleischman's "Fireflies," and just plain fun with Beverly Cleary's Henry and Ribsy. There's truly something for everyone.

I still read animal stories and enjoy them more than ever. Perhaps that is because my love and respect for animals has grown over the years. Animals seem to have the virtues I most admire—courage, loyalty, strength, intelligence, and those traits deep within us all—a love of freedom and a zest for life.

Well, obviously I never did become Clyde Beatty. I never got the chance to show my skills in the depths of the jungle or under the bright lights of the big top. But I can offer you what I longed for most of all in those days —an entrance into the magical world of animals.

Lloyd Alexander

THE RASCAL CROW

EDWYN, ANCIENT GUARDIAN and protector of animals, one day sent urgent word for the birds and beasts to join in council with him. So from lair and burrow, nest and hive, proud stag and humble mole, bright-winged eagle and drab wren, they hastened to his valley. No human could have found or followed the secret path to this shelter, for only creatures of field and forest had knowledge of it.

There they gathered, every kind and degree, one from each clan and tribe. Before them stood Medwyn garbed in a coarse brown robe, his white beard reaching to his waist, his white hair about his shoulders, his only ornament a golden band, set with a blue gem, circling his weathered brow. He spread his gnarled and knotted arms in welcome to the waiting council.

"You know, all of you," he began, in a clear voice unweakened by his years, "long ago, when the dark waters flooded Prydain, I built a ship and carried your forefathers here to safety. Now I must warn you: your own lives are threatened."

Hearing this, the animals murmured and twittered in dismay. But Kadwyr the crow flapped his glossy wings, clacked his beak, and gaily called out:

"What, more wind and water? Let the ducks have the joy of it! Don't worry about me. My nest is high and strong enough. I'll stay where I am. Good sailing to all web-feet!"

Chuckling, making loud, impudent quackings at the blue teal, Kadwyr would have flown off then and there. Medwyn summoned him back, saying:

"Ah, Kadwyr, you're as great a scamp as your grand-sire who sailed with me. No, it is neither flood nor storm. The danger is far worse. King Arawn, Lord of the Land of Death, seeks to enslave all you forest creatures, to break you to his will and bind you to serve his evil ends. Those cousins to the eagles, the gentle gwythaints, have already fallen prey to him. Arawn has lured them to his realm and trapped them in iron cages. Alas, they are beyond our help. We can only grieve for them.

"Take warning from their fate," Medwyn continued. "For now the Death-Lord sends his Chief Huntsman to bait and snare you, to bring you captive to the Land of Death or to slaughter you without mercy. Together you must set your plans to stand against him."

"A crow's a match for any hunter," said Kadwyr. "Watch your step, the rest of you, especially you slow-footed cud-chewers."

Medwyn sighed and shook his head at the brash crow. "Even you, Kadwyr, may be glad for another's help."

Kadwyr only shrugged his wings and cocked a bold eye at Edyrnion the eagle, who flew to perch on Medwyn's outstretched arm.

"Friend of eagles," Edyrnion said, "I and my kinsmen will keep watch from the sky. Our eyes are keen, our wings are swift. At first sight of the hunter, we will spread the alarm."

"Mind you, don't fly too close to the sun," put in Kadwyr with a raucous chuckle. "You'll singe your pin-feathers and moult ahead of season. If there's any watching needed, I'd best be the one to do it. I hear you're going a bit nearsighted these days."

The nimble crow hopped away before the eagle could

call him to account for his teasing. And now the gray wolf Brynach came to crouch at Medwyn's feet, saying:

"Friend of wolves, I and my kinsmen will range the forest. Our teeth are sharp, our jaws are strong. Should the hunter come among us, let him beware of our wolf packs."

"And you'd better watch out for that long tail of yours," said Kadwyr. "With all your dashing back and forth, you're likely to get burrs in it. In fact, you might do well to leave all that roving and roaming to me. My beak's as sharp as any wolf's tooth. And," the crow added, winking, "I never have to stop and scratch fleas."

The wolf's golden eyes flashed and he looked ready to teach the crow a lesson in manners. But he kept his temper and sat back on his haunches as Gwybeddin the gnat flew close to Medwyn's ear and bravely piped up:

"Friend of gnats! We are a tiny folk, but we mean to do our best in any way we can."

Hearing this, Kadwyr squawked with laughter and called out to the gnat:

"Is that you, Prince Flyspeck? I can hardly see you. Listen, old friend, the best thing you can do is hide in a dust cloud, and no hunter will ever find you. Why, even your words are bigger than you are!"

Kadwyr's remarks so embarrassed the poor gnat that he blushed and buzzed away as fast as he could. Meantime, Nedir the spider had clambered up to Medwyn's sleeve, where she clung with her long legs, and declared:

"Friend of spiders! We spinners and weavers are craftsmen, not fighters. But we shall give our help gladly wherever it is needed."

"Take my advice, Granny," Kadwyr said with a chuckle, "and keep to your knitting. Be careful you don't get your arms and legs mixed up, or you'll never untangle them."

Kadwyr hopped about and flirted his tailfeathers, croaking and cackling as the other creatures came forward one by one. The owl declared that he and his fellows would serve as night watch. The fox vowed to use his cunning to baffle the hunter and lead him on false trails. The bees pledged to wield their stings as swords and daggers. The bears offered their strength, the stags their speed, and the badgers their courage to protect their neighbors and themselves.

Last of all, plodding under his heavy burden, came Crugan-Crawgan the turtle.

"Friend of turtles," began Crugan-Crawgan in a halting voice, pondering each word, "I came . . . yes, well, that is to say I, ah, started . . . in all possible haste . . ."

"And we'll be well into next week by the time you've done telling us," Kadwyr said impatiently.

"We are . . . as I should be the first to admit . . . we are, alas, neither swift nor strong. But if I might be allowed . . . ah, permitted to state . . . we're solid. Very, very . . . solid. And . . . steady."

"Have done!" cried Kadwyr, hopping onto the turtle's shell. "You'll put me to sleep! The safest thing you can do is stay locked up in that portable castle of yours. Pull in your head! Tuck in your tail! I'll see to it the hunter doesn't batter down your walls. By the way, old fellow, didn't you have a race with a snail the other day? Tell me, who won?"

"Oh, that," replied Crugan-Crawgan. "Yes, Kadwyr, you see, what happened . . ."

Kadwyr did not wait for the turtle's answer, for Medwyn now declared the council ended, and the crow flapped away, laughing and cackling to himself. "Gnats and spiders! Turtles! What an army! I'll have to keep an eye on all of them."

Once in the forest, however, Kadwyr gave little thought to Medwyn's warning. The beavers toiled at making their dams into strongholds; the squirrels stopped up the crannies in their hollow trees; the moles dug deeper tunnels and galleries. Though every creature offered him shelter in case of need, Kadwyr shook his glossy head and answered:

"Not for me, those holes and burrows! Wits and

wings! Wings and wits! There's not a crow hatched who can't get the best of any hunter!"

Soon Edyrnion and his eagle kinsmen came swooping into the forest, beating their wings and spreading the alarm. The wolf packs leaped from their lairs, the bears from their dens, the foxes from their earths, gathering to join battle against the hunter; and all the forest dwellers, each in his own way, made ready to defend nest and bower, cave and covert.

Kadwyr, however, perched on a branch, rocking back and forth, whistling gaily, daring the invader to catch him. While the smaller, weaker animals hid silent and fearful, Kadwyr hopped up and down, cawing at the top of his voice. And before the crow knew it, the hunter sprang from a thicket.

Garbed in the skins of slain animals, a long knife at his belt, a bow and quiver of arrows slung over his shoulder, the hunter had come so stealthily that Kadwyr scarcely had a moment to collect his wits. The hunter flung out a net so strong and finely woven that once caught in it, no creature could hope to struggle free.

But Kadwyr's eye was quicker than the hunter's snare. With a taunting cackle the crow hopped into the air, flapped his wings, and flew from the branch to perch higher in the tree, where he peered down and brazenly waggled his tailfeathers.

Leaving his net, with a snarl of anger the hunter unslung his bow, fitted an arrow to the string, and sent the shaft hissing straight for the crow.

Chuckling, Kadwyr fluttered his wings and sailed out of the path of the speeding arrow; then turned back to dance in the air in front of the furious hunter, who drew the bow again and again. Swooping and soaring, the crow dodged every shaft.

Seeing the hunter's quiver almost empty, Kadwyr grew even bolder, gliding closer, circling beyond reach, then swooping back to liven the game again. Gnashing his teeth at the elusive prey, the hunter struck out wildly, trying to seize the nimble crow.

Kadwyr sped away. As he flew, he turned his head in a backward glance to jeer at his defeated pursuer. In that heedless instant, the crow collided with a tree trunk.

Stunned, Kadwyr plummeted to the ground. The hunter ran toward him. Kadwyr croaked in pain as he strove to fly to safety. But his wing hung useless at his side, broken.

Breathless, Kadwyr scrambled into the bushes. The hunter plunged after him. Earthbound and wounded, Kadwyr began wishing he had not been so quick to turn down shelter from the squirrels and beavers. With the hunter gaining on him, the crow gladly would have squeezed into any tunnel, or burrow, or rabbit hole he could find. But all had been sealed, blocked, and barred with stones and twigs.

Dragging his wing, the crow skittered through the underbrush. His spindly legs were ill-suited to running, and he longed for the swiftness of the hare. He stumbled and went sprawling. An arrow buried itself in the ground beside him.

The hunter drew his bow. Though this was his pursuer's last arrow, Kadwyr knew himself a helpless target. Only a few paces away, the hunter took aim.

That same instant, a cloud of dust came whirling through the trees. Expecting in another moment to be skewered, Kadwyr now saw the hunter fling up his arms and drop his bow. The arrow clattered harmlessly into the leaves. Next, Kadwyr was sure his opponent had lost his wits. Roaring with pain, the hunter waved his arms and beat his hands against his face, trying to fend off the cloud buzzing about his head and shoulders.

The host of gnats swarmed over the raging hunter, darted into his ears and eyes, streamed up his nose and out his mouth. The more the hunter swept away the tiny creatures, the more they set upon him.

"Gwybeddin!" burst out the crow as one of the swarm broke from the cloud and lit on his beak. "Thank you for my life! Did I call you a flyspeck? You and your gnats are brave as eagles!"

"Hurry!" piped the gnat. "We're doing all we can, but he's more than a match for us. Quick, away with you!"

Kadwyr needed no urging. The gnats had saved him from the hunter's arrows and, as well, had let him snatch a moment's rest. The crow set off again as fast as he could scramble through the dry leaves and dead branches of the forest floor.

Brave though Gwybeddin and his fellows had been, their efforts did not keep the hunter long from the chase. Soon Kadwyr heard footfalls crashing close behind him. The hunter had easily found the crow's trail and seemed to gain in strength while his prey weakened with each step.

The crow plunged deeper into the woods, hoping to hide in a heavy growth of brambles or a thicket where the hunter could not follow. Instead, to Kadwyr's dismay, the forest here grew sparser. Before the crow could find cover, the hunter sighted him and gave a triumphant shout.

Not daring another backward glance, Kadwyr scrambled through a grove of trees. The ground before him lay clear and hard-packed; but while the way was easier for him, he realized it was easier, too, for his enemy to overtake him.

Just then Kadwyr heard a bellow of rage. The crow halted to see the hunter twisting and turning, struggling as if caught in his own net. Kadwyr stared in amazement. Amid the trees, Nedir and all the spiders in the forest had joined to spin their strongest webs. The strands were so fine the hunter had not seen them, but now they clung to him, twined and wrapped around him, and the more he tried to fight loose, the more they enshrouded him.

From a branch above Kadwyr's head, sliding down a single invisible thread, came Nedir, waving her long legs.

"We spinners and weavers have done our best," she called out, "but even our stoutest webs will soon give way. Be off, while you have the chance!"

"Granny Spider," cried the grateful Kadwyr, "forgive me if I ever made sport of you. Your knitting saved my neck!"

Once again the crow scurried away, sure this time he had escaped for good and all. Despite the pain in his wing, his spirits rose and he began gleefully cackling at the sight of the hunter so enmeshed in a huge cocoon.

But Kadwyr soon snapped his beak shut. His eyes darted about in alarm, for his flight had brought him to the edge of a steep cliff.

He halted and fearfully drew back. Without the use of his wing he would have fallen like a stone and been dashed to pieces on the rocks below. However, before he could decide which way to turn, he saw the hunter racing toward him.

Free of the spiders' webs, more enraged than ever, and bent on making an end of the elusive crow, the hunter pulled his knife from his belt. With a shout of triumph, he sprang at the helpless Kadwyr.

The crow, certain his last moment had come, flapped his one good wing and thrust out his beak, bound that he would sell his life dearly.

But the hunter stumbled in mid-stride. His foot caught on a round stone that tripped him up and sent him plunging headlong over the cliff.

Kadwyr's terror turned to joyous relief. He cawed, cackled, and crowed as loudly as any rooster. Then his beak fell open in astonishment.

The stone that had saved his life began to sprout four stubby legs and a tail; a leathery neck stretched out cautiously, and Crugan-Crawgan, the turtle, blinked at Kadwyr.

"Are you all right?" asked Crugan-Crawgan. "That is, I mean to say . . . you've come to no harm? I'm sorry . . . ah, Kadwyr, there wasn't more I could have . . . done. We turtles, alas, can't run . . . like rabbits. Or fly . . . like eagles. But we are, I hope you'll agree . . . yes, we are solid, if nothing else. And . . . very, very steady."

"Crugan-Crawgan," said Kadwyr, "you saved my life and I thank you. Steady and solid you are, old fellow, and I'm glad of it."

"By the way," the turtle went on, "as I was saying . . . the last time we met. . . . Yes, the snail and I did have a race. It was . . . a draw."

The forest was again safe and the rejoicing animals came out of their hiding places. Edyrnion the eagle bore the wounded crow to Medwyn's valley, to be cared for and sheltered until his wing healed.

"Ah, Kadwyr, you scamp, I didn't expect to see you here so soon," Medwyn told the crow, who admitted all that had happened in the woods. "Your wing will mend and you'll be ready for some new scrape. But let us hope next time you can help your friends as they helped you."

"I know better than to scorn a spider," said Kadwyr, crestfallen. "I'll never taunt a turtle. And never again annoy a gnat. But—but, come to think of it," he went on, his eyes brightening, "if it hadn't been for me—yes, it was I! I who led that hunter a merry chase! I who saved all in the forest!"

Kadwyr chuckled and clucked, bobbed his head, and snapped his beak, altogether delighted with himself.

"Perhaps you did, at that," Medwyn gently answered. "In any case, go in peace, Kadwyr. The world has room enough for a rascal crow."

Beverly Cleary

HENRY AND RIBSY GO FISHING

"I CAN'T FIND my tin pants," Mr. Huggins announced Friday evening after supper.

"Dad!" shouted Henry. When his father got out his tin pants, which were not tin at all but heavy canvas, Henry knew it meant only one thing. His father was going fishing—salmon fishing. "I get to go too, don't I? Don't I, Dad?"

Mr. Huggins grinned at Henry. "Think you can get up at three in the morning?"

"Sure, I'll get up! Boy, oh, boy, I bet I catch a bigger salmon than anybody!"

"I wouldn't count on it," said Mr. Huggins. "I'm afraid a twenty- or thirty-pound Chinook would be too much for you to handle."

"Aw, I bet I could land one," boasted Henry. After all, if he could lift Robert when they practiced tumbling, a twenty-five-pound fish couldn't be so heavy. He could see himself having his picture taken with his salmon in one hand and his rod in the other. Well, maybe he couldn't hold up such a big fish with one hand but he could prop it up some way.

"Henry," Mrs. Huggins looked thoughtfully at her son, "you mustn't be too disappointed if you don't catch anything."

"I won't, Mom, but I just know I'll catch a salmon." Henry patted his dog, who was dozing in front of the fireplace. "Did you hear that, Ribsy? We're going fishing!"

"Hey, who said anything about Ribsy?" asked Mr. Huggins.

"Aw, Dad, he wouldn't be any trouble," protested Henry. "Would you, fellow?" Ribsy opened one eye and looked at Henry.

"If Henry is old enough to go fishing, so is Ribsy," said Mrs. Huggins. Then she smiled and said, "Tomorrow is my vacation. I'll pack your lunches tonight and you can get your own breakfast. I'm going to sleep late and I don't want to have to get up to let Ribsy in and out."

"All right, Ribsy goes fishing," agreed Mr. Huggins.

"Where are we going?" Henry wanted to know.

"I thought we'd try our luck at the mouth of the Umptucca River," answered Henry's father.

"That's where Scooter went last week," remarked Henry.

"Henry, you'd better run along to bed if you're going to get up at three in the morning," said Mrs. Huggins. "And be sure you wear warm clothes tomorrow. It will be cold over on the coast."

For once Henry did not object to going to bed early. Even so, it seemed as if it were still the middle of the night when his father woke him. They could see the stars shining as they ate a hurried breakfast, standing at the draining board. When Ribsy padded into the kitchen to see what was going on, Henry gave him half a can of Woofies and some horse meat.

The Grumbies' screen door slammed. "Get your rain hat and coat and let's go." Mr. Huggins picked up two lunch boxes from the kitchen table and hurried out the back door.

"So you're going with us," said Mr. Grumbie, when he saw Henry.

"Yes, and I bet I catch a salmon," answered Henry.

"Better not count on it," said Mr. Grumbie, and yawned. He frowned when he saw Ribsy getting into the back seat of the Huggins car with Henry, but he yawned again and did not say anything.

As they drove out of the city, Henry listened to his father and Mr. Grumbie talk about fish they had caught on other fishing trips. Ribsy could not decide where he wanted to ride. He jumped from the back seat to the front seat. He walked across Mr. Grumbie's lap and wagged his tail in his face. When Mr. Grumbie did not lower the window for him, Ribsy scrambled into the back seat and bounded from one side of the car to the other, until Henry opened a window so he could lean out and sniff all the interesting smells.

Mr. Grumbie turned around and frowned at Ribsy. He did not say anything. He just turned up the collar of his mackinaw.

"Henry, it's pretty cold for an open window," said Mr. Huggins.

"O.K., Dad." Henry pulled Ribsy back into the car by his collar and wound up the window. Ribsy turned around three times, curled up on the seat, and went to sleep.

Mr. Grumbie told about the big one that got away down on the Nehalem River. I bet I do catch a salmon, Henry thought, and using Ribsy for a pillow he fell asleep himself.

. . .

Henry did not wake up until the car left the highway and began to bounce along a gravel road near a bridge that bore a sign, *Umptucca River*. The sky was gray and the air smelled of the sea. "Is it time for lunch?" Henry asked.

"Here we are," said Mr. Huggins, "and it is exactly six A.M."

Henry got out of the car and looked around. In the dim morning light he could see a shabby building with *Sportsmen's Cannery* painted across the front, a tiny restaurant with steamy windows, a few cabins, and a boathouse with a sign, *Mike's Place. Boats and Tackle.* The sound of the breakers and the sight of the rows of boats bobbing in the river below the boathouse filled Henry with excitement. He was really here. He was really going salmon fishing.

While Mr. Huggins rented a boat, Ribsy ran in circles sniffing all the strange new smells. Henry examined the scales hanging from the eaves of the boathouse. He took hold of the hook and pulled down until the hand of the scales spun around and pointed to twenty-five pounds. It sure takes a lot of pulling to make twenty-five pounds, thought Henry. More than anything he wanted to hang a salmon on that hook and see the hand point to twenty-five—or maybe even thirty. He would have his picture taken with his salmon hanging on the scales so everyone would know how much it weighed.

"I brought my boy along this time," Mr. Huggins said to Mike, the owner of the boathouse.

"Well, hello there, Shorty," said Mike. "So they're going to make a fisherman out of you."

"Yes, sir. I hope I catch a salmon," answered Henry, and when he saw Mike's smile he was sorry he had said it. Maybe everyone was right. Maybe he couldn't land a salmon even if one did bite. Still, there wasn't any harm in hoping he could, was there?

"Fishing pretty good?" asked Mr. Huggins.

"Pretty good," Mike answered. "Fellow brought in a thirty-six-pounder yesterday."

Thirty-six pounds! Oh, boy, thought Henry, as he took the lunches and followed his father and Mr. Grumbie down the steps to a boat tied to a float in the river. Ribsy followed Henry into the boat and sniffed at the lunches.

"Wind from the south. Going to rain," remarked Mr. Grumbie, as he wound the rope around the starter and yanked it. The motor sputtered and was silent. Mr. Grumbie rewound the rope.

Hurry, thought Henry. I want to get started fishing.

Mr. Grumbie yanked the rope again. This time the motor started. Henry turned up the collar of his rain-coat against the wind and hung on to the side of the boat. The river looked cold and deep. Ribsy stood in the bow and barked excitedly at the sea gulls wheeling overhead, as their boat joined the other boats scurrying toward the sand bars at the mouth of the river.

Although the Umptucca was several hundred feet wide at Mike's Place, it was much narrower where it ran into the ocean, because sand bars had formed on either side of the river's mouth. Mr. Grumbie anchored the boat just inside the sand bars in line with the boats already there. Henry knew this was the best spot to catch the fish as they came out of the ocean and started up the river to spawn.

"Golly," said Henry, as he watched the swift current of the river seethe against the breakers, "it looks like the river is fighting to get into the ocean and the ocean is fighting to get into the river. I wouldn't want to fall in and get carried out there."

Mr. Huggins and Mr. Grumbie did not answer. They were too busy getting out the tackle. Mr. Huggins handed Henry a stout rod with a reel attached. The end of the line was fastened to one corner of a three-cornered piece of plastic. A lead sinker was joined to another corner and from the third corner hung a piece of wire with a hook, some red feathers, and a glittering piece of brass.

"Henry, I think the easiest way for you to fish is to drop your line overboard and let the current carry it out," said Mr. Huggins. "Like this." He tossed the line into the water. The reel on the rod began to spin as the line was carried out.

"But you didn't bait the hook," said Henry.

"Salmon that are trying to get up the river to spawn aren't hungry," explained Mr. Huggins. "They bite because the brass spinner makes them angry."

"Oh," said Henry. He hoped he could make a salmon good and angry. Then he said, "Ribsy, you get away from those lunches."

Henry and the two men settled down to fish in silence. Henry dropped his line overboard, let it be carried out, and slowly reeled it in. His father and Mr. Grumbie, skillful fishermen, threw their lines out.

Henry dropped his line again and again. The wind grew colder and his nose began to run. Toss out the line, reel it in, wipe his nose. Toss out the line, reel it in, wipe his nose. Finally he said, "Dad, is it lunchtime yet?"

Mr. Huggins looked at his watch. "It is exactly eight thirty-six."

Toss out the line, reel it in, wipe his nose. Henry tried not to think about how hungry he was. Ribsy sniffed at the lunches and looked hopefully at Henry.

A shout went up from another boat, and Henry looked in time to see a man lean out of his boat and hook a great silvery fish through the gills with his gaff and pull it into his boat.

"Must be a twenty-pounder," remarked Mr. Grumbie, as the line sang from his reel.

Henry was filled with excitement at the sight of the great fish. Come on, salmon, bite, he thought, and tossed out his line.

Large raindrops began to splash the boat. Then the rain came pelting down. Rivulets of water ran off Henry's rain hat. Ribsy shivered and whimpered. Toss out the line, reel it in, wipe his nose. Henry began to wonder if salmon fishing was so much fun after all. If only he was not so hungry.

Finally when the rain stopped Mr. Huggins said, "What do you say we knock off for a few minutes and have a sandwich?"

"Suits me," said Mr. Grumbie.

"Boy, am I starved!" Henry reached for his lunch box. He poured some soup from his thermos and bit into a thick ham sandwich. Mmm, did it taste good! Ribsy watched every bite he took. When Henry swallowed, Ribsy swallowed. Poor Ribsy. He looked so thin with his wet hair plastered against his body. Henry gave him half a sandwich.

"Save some lunch for later," warned Mr. Huggins. "We have a long day ahead of us."

Ribsy gulped the bread and meat. Then he stood up and shook himself so hard his license tags jingled. Water showered in every direction, spattering faces, soaking sandwiches, splashing into the coffee the men were drinking from their thermos tops.

"Hey, cut that out!" Mr. Huggins tried to hold his sandwich out of the spray.

Mr. Grumbie did not say anything. When Ribsy stopped shaking, he pulled out a handkerchief and mopped his face. Then he poured his coffee into the river, stuffed his sandwich back into his lunch box, and got out another.

Mr. Grumbie sure is fussy, thought Henry, taking a big bite out of his soggy sandwich, while Ribsy sat in front of him and watched hungrily. He wagged his tail to show he would like another bite. His tail slapped against the tackle box. Before Henry could grab it, the box turned over, spilling spinners, hooks, and sinkers into the water in the bottom of the boat.

"That sure was close," exclaimed Henry, looking at the tangle of tackle. "Ribsy might have got a fishhook in his tail. That would have been awful."

Mr. Grumbie cleared his throat. "Uh, yes," he said, and bent to unsnarl the tackle.

"Henry," said Mr. Huggins quietly, "you'd better keep an eye on Ribsy."

"I'm sorry, Dad." Henry felt uncomfortable. Of

course Mr. Grumbie didn't like Ribsy's overturning the tackle box. But just the same it would have been awful if Ribsy had got a fishhook in his tail.

Henry looked at his wet dog shivering in the wind. "Here, Ribsy, get under my raincoat." He made a place for Ribsy, who managed to turn around three times before he curled up on the narrow seat and went to sleep. At least he can't get into trouble when he's asleep, thought Henry, and wolfed a third sandwich, the rest of his soup, a deviled egg, a piece of chocolate cake, and a banana.

The warm soup and the rocking of the boat made Henry sleepy. He tossed out his line, reeled it in, and wiped his nose over and over again. Why couldn't a fish hurry up and bite? He wished he could go back to the boathouse and stretch his legs, but he didn't like to say so when his father and Mr. Grumbie were so interested in fishing. Occasionally a shout went up from one of the other boats and someone held up a salmon. Rain clouds washed over the forest-covered mountains along the edge of the sea. To the south Henry could see another shower approaching. He turned up the collar of his raincoat and waited for the first drops to come spattering down.

"What time is it, Dad?" Henry asked.

"Ten o'clock," answered his father, reeling in his line. "Getting tired?"

"N-no." Henry tried to keep from shivering. Only ten o'clock in the morning. It seemed as if they had been there forever. Why, it wasn't even lunchtime! If only he could put his head down someplace for just a few minutes . . .

Suddenly Mr. Grumbie uttered a noise that sounded like "Wup!"

"Got something?" Mr. Huggins' voice was tense as he put down his rod and picked up the gaff.

"Yup." Grimly Mr. Grumbie wound his reel.

Henry was no longer sleepy. He dropped his rod and watched eagerly as Mr. Grumbie reeled in his line. He wanted to see exactly how a fish was landed. If a salmon bit for Mr. Grumbie, a salmon might bite for him.

Mr. Grumbie stopped winding the reel. The line began to unwind and Henry knew the salmon was pulling on it. "Is it going to get away?" Henry whispered to his father. He knew he must not disturb Mr. Grumbie.

"I don't think so," answered Mr. Huggins. "If the fish puts up a fight, it's best to let him have the line or he'll break it."

When Mr. Grumbie began to wind the reel again, Henry watched breathlessly. Suddenly the fish began to fight once more. Mr. Grumbie looked grim as he waited for the salmon to rest. Then he turned the handle of the reel again. The great fish flopped out of the water near the boat. "Get him!" said Mr. Grumbie.

Henry watched his father lean out of the boat with the gaff. "Got him," he said, as he hooked the fish through the gills and yanked it into the boat. The enormous fish did not stop fighting. Mr. Huggins tried to club it but missed, and the flopping salmon slapped against the sleeping Ribsy.

Ribsy woke up, saw the strange flopping thing, gave one terrified yelp, and tried to scramble away from it. As he fell over the line and fought desperately to get away, the hook was torn from the salmon's mouth. Mr. Grumbie tried to grab his fish, but it slid through his hands, leaving them covered with scales. Again it slapped against Ribsy, who fell over the lunch boxes in his struggle to get away. With one mighty flop the fish cleared the side of the boat, landed with a splash that showered Henry and the two men, and swam away.

"Ki-yi-yi," yelped the terrified Ribsy, as he fought free of fishing rods and lunch boxes. With one frantic glance backward, he leaped out of the other side of the boat and started swimming upstream.

It all happened so fast that Henry and the two men sat with their mouths open.

"Well . . ." said Mr. Huggins.

Mr. Grumbie did not say a word. He looked at his

hands, covered with fish scales, and stared at the water where his fish had disappeared.

"Dad, start the boat," yelled Henry. "Get Ribsy. He'll be carried out to sea."

It seemed to Henry that it took his father forever to pull up the anchor and wind the rope around the starter. "Ribsy!" he called frantically to his dog, who was fighting against the swift current of the river with his nose pointed out of the water. "Dad, hurry!" Henry knew that if Ribsy was carried into the breakers he wouldn't have a chance.

Mr. Huggins jerked the rope. The motor sputtered and died. Hurriedly he rewound the rope.

"Dad!" cried Henry in despair. "Ribsy!" The dog was swimming with all his strength but was slowly being carried backward. A gust of wind blew across the choppy water and a wave washed over Ribsy's head.

Still the boat would not start.

"Dad, he can't swim against that current," cried Henry, looking back at the hungry breakers. "Can't you hurry?"

Mr. Huggins rewound the rope and yanked. The motor gave a tired gasp.

Now Ribsy was being carried back past the boat. I've got to get him, thought Henry, and leaned out of the boat. Ribsy was so close he could see the wild look in his eyes and watch his paws working under the water. Henry leaned a little farther out of the boat, reached toward Ribsy, and lost his balance. As he started to topple into the water he felt a hand grab him by the collar of his raincoat and yank him back into the boat.

"Don't lean out," said Mr. Huggins sharply, and re-wound the rope. Henry knew there was no reason now to lean out of the boat. The current had swept Ribsy far beyond his reach.

By this time the fishermen in the other boats were watching. "Don't worry, sonny," called one of the men. He pulled up his anchor, started his powerful motor, and headed toward Ribsy. More terrified than ever by the roar of the motor, Ribsy struggled to get away from the boat bearing down on him.

Henry was almost afraid to look. What if the man couldn't catch Ribsy? Or what if the boat ran over him? The man steered his boat close to Ribsy, reached out with his gaff, hooked it through Ribsy's collar, and lifted the struggling, dripping dog into his boat.

The other fishermen began to laugh. "Must be a thirty-pounder you just landed," someone called.

Henry was limp with relief. Let them laugh. Ribsy was safe. He wasn't going to be carried out into those angry breakers. That was all that mattered.

The man swung his boat around in a wide circle and pulled up close to the Huggins' boat. He handed the soggy dog across to Henry.

"Gee, thanks," Henry managed to say, as he clutched the shivering Ribsy.

"Don't mention it," answered the man. His big boat roared away, leaving the smaller boat bobbing in its wake.

"Gee . . ." Henry hugged his dog. Ribsy licked his face with his long pink tongue. "Gee, that sure was close."

"It sure was," agreed Mr. Huggins. An uncomfortable silence fell on all three. "Sorry about the salmon, Grumbie," added Mr. Huggins.

"Must have been a twenty-five-pounder," said Mr. Grumbie regretfully.

Henry didn't want to look at Mr. Grumbie. "I'm sorry too," he said, as he ran his hand along Ribsy's tail to wipe off some of the water. "I guess Ribsy had never seen a salmon before and it scared him. I know he didn't mean to make you lose it."

"Henry, how would you like to take Ribsy to the boathouse to dry out?" asked his father.

"Good idea," said Mr. Grumbie.

"O.K., Dad," agreed Henry, because he wanted to get his dog warm and dry again. But from the way Mr. Grumbie spoke he knew he would have to stay there the rest of the day. And his chance to catch a salmon was gone. Henry looked sadly at his dog.

Ribsy stood up and shook himself until his license tags jingled.

(Note: "Henry and Ribsy Go Fishing" is taken from Chapter 6 of *Henry and Ribsy*.)

Virginia Hamilton

HE LION, BRUH BEAR, AND BRUH RABBIT

SAY THAT HE Lion would get up each and every mornin. Stretch and walk around. He'd roar, "ME AND MYSELF. ME AND MYSELF," like that. Scare all the little animals so they were afraid to come outside in the sunshine. Afraid to go huntin or fishin or whatever the little animals wanted to do.

"What we gone do about it?" they asked one another. Squirrel leapin from branch to branch, just scared. Possum playin dead, couldn't hardly move him.

He Lion just went on, stickin out his chest and roarin, "ME AND MYSELF. ME AND MYSELF."

The little animals held a sit-down talk, and one by one and two by two and all by all, they decide to go see Bruh Bear and Bruh Rabbit. For they know that Bruh Bear been around. And Bruh Rabbit say he has, too.

So they went to Bruh Bear and Bruh Rabbit. Said, "We have some trouble. Old he Lion, him scarin everybody, roarin every mornin and all day, 'ME AND MYSELF. ME AND MYSELF,' like that."

"Why he Lion want to do that?" Bruh Bear said.

"Is that all he Lion have to say?" Bruh Rabbit asked.

"We don't know why, but that's all he Lion can tell us and we didn't ask him to tell us that," said the little animals. "And him scarin the children with it. And we wish him to stop it."

"Well, I'll go see him, talk to him. I've known he Lion a long kind of time," Bruh Bear said.

"I'll go with you," said Bruh Rabbit. "I've known he Lion most long as you."

That bear and that rabbit went off through the forest. They kept hearin somethin. Mumble, mumble. Couldn't make it out. They got farther in the forest. They heard it plain now. "ME AND MYSELF. ME AND MYSELF."

"Well, well, well," said Bruh Bear. He wasn't scared. He'd been around the whole forest, seen a lot.

"My, my, my," said Bruh Rabbit. He'd seen enough to know not to be afraid of an old he lion. Now old he lions could be dangerous, but you had to know how to handle them.

The bear and the rabbit climbed up and up the cliff where he Lion had his lair. They found him. Kept their distance. He watchin them and they watchin him. Everybody actin cordial.

"Hear tell you are scarin everybody, all the little animals, with your roarin all the time," Bruh Rabbit said.

"I roars when I pleases," he Lion said.

"Well, might could you leave off the noise first thing in the mornin, so the little animals can get what they want to eat and drink?" asked Bruh Bear.

"Listen," said he Lion, and then he roared: "ME AND MYSELF. ME AND MYSELF. Nobody tell me what not to do," he said. "I'm the king of the forest, *me and myself.*"

"Better had let me tell you somethin," Bruh Rabbit said, "for I've seen Man, and I know him the real king of the forest."

He Lion was quiet awhile. He looked straight through that scrawny lil Rabbit like he was nothin atall. He looked at Bruh Bear and figured he'd talk to him.

"You, Bear, you been around," he Lion said.

"That's true," said old Bruh Bear. "I been about everywhere. I've been around the whole forest."

"Then you must know somethin," he Lion said.

"I know lots," said Bruh Bear, slow and quiet-like.

"Tell me what you know about Man," he Lion said. "He think him the king of the forest?"

"Well, now, I'll tell you," said Bruh Bear, "I been around, but I haven't ever come across Man that I know of. Couldn't tell you nothin about him."

So he Lion had to turn back to Bruh Rabbit. He didn't want to but he had to. "So what?" he said to that lil scrawny hare.

"Well, you got to come down from there if you want to see Man," Bruh Rabbit said. "Come down from there and I'll show you him."

He Lion thought a minute, an hour, and a whole day. Then, the next day, he came on down.

He roared just once, "ME AND MYSELF. ME AND MYSELF. Now," he said, "come show me Man."

So they set out. He Lion, Bruh Bear, and Bruh Rabbit. They go along and they go along, rangin the forest. Pretty soon, they come to a clearin. And playin in it is a little fellow about nine years old.

"Is that there Man?" asked he Lion.

"Why no, that one is called Will Be, but it sure is not Man," said Bruh Rabbit.

So they went along and they went along. Pretty soon, they come upon a shade tree. And sleepin under it is an old, olden fellow, about ninety years olden.

"There must lie Man," spoke he Lion. "I knew him wasn't gone be much."

"That's not Man," said Bruh Rabbit. "That fellow is Was Once. You'll know it when you see Man."

So they went on along. He Lion is gettin tired of strollin. So he roars, "ME AND MYSELF. ME AND MYSELF." Upsets Bear so that Bear doubles over and runs and climbs a tree.

"Come down from there," Bruh Rabbit tellin him. So after a while Bear comes down. He keepin his distance from he Lion, anyhow. And they set out some more. Goin along quiet and slow.

In a little while they come to a road. And comin on way down the road, Bruh Rabbit sees Man comin. Man about twenty-one years old. Big and strong, with a big gun over his shoulder.

"There!" Bruh Rabbit says. "See there, he Lion? There's Man. You better go meet him."

"I will," says he Lion. And he sticks out his chest and he roars, "ME AND MYSELF. ME AND MYSELF." All the way to Man he's roarin proud, "ME AND MYSELF, ME AND MYSELF!"

"Come on, Bruh Bear, let's go!" Bruh Rabbit says.

"What for?" Bruh Bear wants to know.

"You better come on!" And Bruh Rabbit takes ahold of Bruh Bear and half drags him to a thicket. And there he makin the Bear hide with him.

For here comes Man. He sees old he Lion real good now. He drops to one knee and he takes aim with his big gun.

Old he Lion is roarin his head off: "ME AND MYSELF! ME AND MYSELF!"

The big gun goes off: PA-LOOOM!

He Lion falls back hard on his tail.

The gun goes off again. PA-LOOOM!

He Lion is flyin through the air. He lands in the thicket.

"Well, did you see Man?" asked Bruh Bear.

"I seen him," said he Lion. "Man spoken to me un-kind, and got a great long stick him keepin on his shoulder. Then Man taken that stick down and him speakin real mean. Thunderin at me and lightnin comin from that stick, awful bad. Made me sick. I had to turn around. And Man pointin that stick again and thunderin at me some more. So I come in here, cause it seem like him throwed some stickers at me each time it thunder, too."

"So you've met Man, and you know zactly what that kind of him is," says Bruh Rabbit.

"I surely do know that," he Lion said back.

Awhile after he Lion met Man, things were some better in the forest. Bruh Bear knew what Man looked like so he could keep out of his way. That rabbit always did know to keep out of Man's way. The little animals could go out in the mornin because he Lion was more peaceable. He didn't walk around roarin at the top of his voice all the time. And when he Lion did lift that voice of his, it was like, "Me and Myself and Man. Me and Myself and Man." Like that.

Wasn't too loud atall.

———■———

Animal tales are the most widely known black folktales. Because of the menial labor slaves were made to do, they observed and came to know many kinds of animals throughout their daily lives. They developed a keen interest in these lowly creatures. Because they had so little knowledge about the fauna they found here, they made up tales that to some extent explained and fit their observations of animal behavior. Furthermore, the tales satisfied the slaves' need to explain symbolically and secretly the ruling behavior of the slaveowners in relation to themselves. As time passed, the tales were told more for entertainment and instruction.

"He Lion, Bruh Bear, and Bruh Rabbit" is a typical tale of an animal, whether it is wolf, lion, bear, rabbit, goat, tiger, etc., that learns through experience to fear man. It is the rabbit that shows man to the lion. And the rabbit, representing the slave in the animal tales, knows from experience to fear man. The tale ranges throughout North and South America, Europe, and Africa.

Will James

TOM AND JERRY

I'VE OFTEN SEEN ponies pair off, form a partnership and stick by themselves, and they'd fight for one another when there was a need to.

That's the kind of partners Tom and Jerry were. Maybe it was because they were full brothers but anyway they were sure *for* one another. By their color and markings and size you could hardly tell them apart. Both were blood bays with one white hind foot and a star in the forehead. And in the way they acted they were alike, too.

I paid twenty dollars for them when they were two-year-olds. Tom was four and Jerry was five when I started breaking them in. I found them both wiry and full of snorts, and between the two of them I got many a good shaking up. But when I got through with them I had two more good horses to my string of private saddle horses.

I'd always noticed that when I turned them out on the range with the other horses they never seemed to want to run with any bunch. Instead they'd always go by themselves and I never failed to find them all by their lonesome, never more than a few feet apart.

But I had no idea how strong their partnership really was until one spring when I'd hunted high and low for them and couldn't find them. I'd got to thinking they'd left the country and gone back to their home range, which was more than a hundred miles away. Then one day, as I was riding along watching for them, I saw a lone horse in the bottom of a coulee. He was running around in small circles and seemed to be chasing something. I couldn't make out just what he was chasing. I was too far away to tell. The thing he was chasing would always turn around and come back to the place where the lone horse made his stand.

I kept a low ridge between me and the spot where I'd seen the lone horse and rode on to where I thought I'd be as close as I could get without being seen. Then I rode for the ridge straight to where things were happening.

I didn't ride over the ridge but just so I could see over it. I found that the lone horse was Jerry and then I saw what he was chasing. It was a big gray wolf. Right away I could see that Jerry was tired out and the wolf knew he couldn't fight much longer.

If I'd had my rifle with me I could have shot the wolf. I was too far for a sure shot with my six-shooter, but, as I got off my horse and dragged myself through the tall grass, I hoped the wolf would keep on being interested in Jerry just long enough so I could get near.

Where could Tom be? I wondered, as I eased myself towards Jerry and the wolf. Then I thought how queer Jerry was acting. Every time he'd chase the wolf away he'd come back and stand in one spot as if waiting for him to come again. If the wolf came too close the little horse would make a high dive for him with flying hoofs, ears set back and teeth showing.

Jerry was nearly all in, every hair on him was wet with sweat and from the way he looked I knew he hadn't had water for a couple of days or more. He hadn't eaten anything either, for a horse that's real thirsty doesn't hanker for grass.

What was it that kept him from leaving that spot and going to water? I wondered, but my wondering was cut short by the wolf. He'd got wind of me when I was about a hundred yards from him, and he threw up his head, sniffed the air and started traveling.

My forty-five spoke to him. Mister Wolf jumped in the air a good six feet and when he landed I let another shot go his way. I fired at him till my gun was empty and each shot only seemed to make him go faster. When I straightened up and watched him go over a hill I thought I saw him dragging one useless front leg.

Jerry was shaking like a leaf. The shots surprised and scared him but he was still in that one spot when I started towards him. I kept watching him to see what was the matter and the closer I got the more that little horse acted glad to see me.

He'd nicker softly, look down to one side of the spot where he'd been standing, then look at me again.

I got to him as fast as I could. As soon as I got there I saw the reason why Jerry hadn't tried to get away from the wolf, why he'd got along without water or feed and why he'd stayed, fought, and protected that spot so long. A hole had been washed out by the snow waters and in that hole, lying on his back, feet in the air and very helpless was Tom—Jerry's partner.

I figured that Tom had been taking a roll and he'd picked a bad place for the purpose. When he rolled over he was too close to the edge of the hole and down in it he went. The more he tried to get out of the hole the more he found himself wedged in to stay.

A horse can't live very long in that unnatural position, so I didn't waste much time. I made a run for the saddle horse I'd left on the ridge, and, with my rope and his strength, I soon got Tom out and right side up.

All the time Jerry was watching me, and when I finally got Tom's feet under him, he came to him, sniffed along Tom's mane and nickered. Tom nickered back.

I couldn't do any more to help them so I just sat there on the edge of the bank. I watched the two ponies and thought a lot. I noticed Jerry staggering for want of water. He'd fought hard and long to save his partner from the wolf, and now that all danger was over he was weak.

He stood there by Tom and *waited* for him to get on his feet so they could both go to the creek together— the creek was only a mile or so away. Pretty soon Tom showed signs of interest in life and tried to get on his feet. I was right there to help him all I could, and after a while Tom managed to stand on his legs. Mighty weak, of course, but sure enough standing.

After that it was just a case of waiting, then Tom took one step, then another.

Jerry watched him and when Tom showed he was

going to keep on going, Jerry caught up with him. Both a-staggering, they headed down the coulee towards the creek.

"Yep," I said to myself as I watched the ponies move away—"and Tom would have done the same for Jerry, too."

Paul Fleischman

FIREFLIES

The following poem is a poem for two voices. It was written to be read aloud by two readers at once, one taking the left-hand part, the other taking the right-hand part. Both readers should read from top to bottom, the two parts meshing as in a musical duet. Lines on the same horizontal level should be spoken simultaneously.

Light	Light
	is the ink we use

Paul Fleischman

Night   Night
is our parchment

                    We're
                    fireflies
fireflies   flickering
flitting

                    flashing
fireflies
glimmering   fireflies
                    gleaming
glowing
Insect calligraphers   Insect calligraphers
practicing penmanship

                    copying sentences
Six-legged scribblers Six-legged scribblers
of vanishing messages,

                    fleeting graffiti
Fine artists in flight Fine artists in flight
adding dabs of light

                    bright brush strokes
Signing the June nights Signing the June nights
as if they were paintings as if they were paintings
                    We're
flickering   fireflies
fireflies   flickering
fireflies.   fireflies.

Robert Lawson

MR. WILMER'S
STRANGE
SATURDAY

WILLIAM WILMER WAS twenty-
nine years old before he discovered that
he could converse with animals. In fact it
happened on his twenty-ninth birthday and it made a
great difference in his life. From then on, life became
highly exciting and lots of fun. He was always a little
sorry that he hadn't discovered his great gift sooner,
because up to that time existence had been very dull
indeed. However, as Mrs. Keeler, his landlady, always
said—especially when she looked at her husband—

"You can't expect everything," so Mr. Wilmer was quite content with the way things worked out.

William Wilmer's twenty-ninth birthday (it came on the nineteenth of April) started just the same as any other day. In fact each of his days, except Sunday, started just the same as every other day, and ended about the same. He wouldn't have remembered that it *was* his birthday, except that in the morning he had received the usual greeting card from his Aunt Edna in Peoria—Aunt Edna never failed to send one. There was always a picture of a bunch of flowers printed on it and the words Birthday Greetings to a Dear Nephew. And written in purple ink there was always the same message: *"You see I never forget, just like the elephant, ha! ha! Your loving* Aunt Edna.*"*

Sometimes Mr. Wilmer wished she *would* forget, just for a change; and having once seen a snapshot of Aunt Edna he thought the elephant simile was rather unwisely chosen. However, he dutifully removed last year's card from the mirror over his bureau and stuck up the new one, where it would remain until next birthday.

This morning, just as every other morning, Mr. Wilmer walked three blocks across town and three blocks down, to where there was a bus stop. It was a beautiful spring morning, quite warm for the nineteenth of April, as Mr. and Mrs. Keeler had both remarked—twice. There had been a shower during the night and now little wisps of steam were rising from the sidewalk wherever the sun struck. An ice wagon rattled by, the driver whistling loudly. A little bird of some sort hopped about in a starved-looking tree and whistled back at him. William Wilmer had a strange, vague feeling that something unusual was stirring in the air today, that today something *different* was going to happen. It disturbed him a little, for he was so used to things being the same that the thought of any change was a bit frightening. "I guess it's just spring," he thought—and, recollecting the birthday card: "After all, twenty-nine isn't so *terribly* old."

The bus took him seven blocks crosstown and twelve down, to the subway station. At the newsstand there, just as every morning, he bought his copy of the *Daily Bleat* and a roll of Peppermint Patooties. On the subway train he sat in his regular front right-hand corner seat of the fourth car, took one Peppermint Patootie, and looked at the pictures of murderers, gunmen and politicians, as far as 72nd Street. At 72nd Street, as usual, he ate his second Patootie and turned to the comic page. There was always just time between 72nd Street and his stop to look at "Captain Super" and "Bring 'em Back Dead," fold the paper and put it in his pocket for Claude the elevator starter, straighten his hat and unwrap three Patooties for the Policeman's horse.

The Policeman always sat on his horse halfway up

the first block from the subway station and for as many mornings as he could remember Mr. Wilmer had always stopped and given the horse three Peppermint Patooties. The horse had learned to recognize him (which few people ever did) and always pawed at the curb and stretched out his neck eagerly at his approach. It was the pleasantest thing in Mr. Wilmer's day; that and saying "Good morning" to that redheaded Miss Sweeney who sat four desks away from him at the office.

The Policeman had never appeared to notice Mr. Wilmer. He always sat up very straight, glaring at the traffic, but this morning he suddenly turned down a beefy, unpleasant face and growled, "Leave off feedin' the horse sugar."

Mr. Wilmer was stunned and quite terrified. It was the first time in his life that a Policeman had ever spoken to him. He could feel little prickles run up his spine, he burst into a sweat and his knees felt weak. He was conscious of the horse's whiskers tickling his hand, of the warm breath that was making the Patooties soft and sticky. Hastily he snatched back the offending offering and tried to speak, but his voice was husky and not very steady.

"Excuse me," he stammered, "I didn't know. It's—er—they're not really sugar. They're peppermint—er—Peppermint Patooties."

The Policeman had resumed his statue-like pose and was again glaring at the traffic. Without even bothering to look down he rumbled, "Peppermint or spearmint or potaties or patooties or sugar or salt—leave off feedin' the horse, that's all."

Burning with embarrassment William Wilmer stumbled away. His head was buzzing, his hand was stuck up with Peppermint Patooties, but he dared not throw them in the gutter—he remembered the signs: DO NOT LITTER YOUR STREETS. He tried to put them in his pocket, but they only gathered tufts of fuzz and stuck tighter.

As he hastened from the scene of his humiliation he suddenly heard a voice speaking. It was a small voice, very small and far away, but perfectly clear and distinct. "The big, bullnecked, ham-faced, overbearing bully," it was saying, "the stupid, selfish, heavy-bottomed brute! I'll get even with him, I'll fix him—"

Mr. Wilmer glanced back over his shoulder and was astonished to discover that there was no one anywhere near. There were only the Policeman, his red neck bulging over his collar, and the impatiently pawing horse. "That's queer," he thought, but he was so confused and upset that he did not realize how queer it really was.

He hurried into the lobby of the Safe, Sane and Colossal Insurance Company Building, forgot to give

Claude the starter his copy of the *Daily Bleat*, and was rewarded for his thoughtlessness by having the elevator door slammed on his heel.

Ever since he had finished High School eleven years ago, William Wilmer had worked for the Safe, Sane and Colossal Insurance Company. The office where he spent his days was on the ninth floor of the S. S. & C. Building. It was a huge room, almost a block square and filled with rows of desks, very much like a schoolroom. There were seventeen aisles and six desks in each row between the aisles. Mr. Wilmer's desk was in the seventh row, second from the left of Aisle J. On each desk was either a typewriter or a calculating machine. Mr. Wilmer's desk had a calculator.

At night the machines were protected by covers of rubberized cloth and every morning punctually at 8:57 William Wilmer sat down at his desk, took off the cover, folded it neatly and placed it in the lower right-hand drawer of his desk. Then he pulled up his cuffs, eased his coat and started to work.

On the right-hand corner of his desk there was always waiting a square wire basket filled with long slips of pink, green or yellow paper on which were columns of figures. The figures on the pink slips were to be added, those on the green slips to be divided and the yellow ones subtracted. So all day Mr. Wilmer punched at the keys of his machine, adding, subtracting or dividing. The results came out on strips of white paper which he carefully placed in a wire basket on the *left*-hand corner of his desk. Punctually, every hour, an office boy brought a fresh basketful of pink, green and yellow slips and carried away the white ones. At 4:57 each afternoon a buzzer sounded, Mr. Wilmer pulled down his cuffs and coat sleeves, put the cover on his machine and went home.

It was not a very exciting life.

The only exciting thing was when he smiled good morning to that redheaded Miss Sweeney who sat four desks to the right of him across Aisle J. Her hair, although undeniably red, was soft and wavy. It looked as though it had been brushed a great deal, not just kinked up with cheap permanents like that of most of the other girls. Her eyes were deep blue, with black-lashed rims, and when she smiled her nose, which was extremely short, wrinkled in a most entrancing way. Her morning greeting made William Wilmer feel warm and happy for hours. He could punch cheerily at the keys of his machine and forget all about the Safe, Sane and Colossal Insurance Company and Mrs. Keeler's tiresome boardinghouse. He didn't quite know just what he *did* think about at those times, but they were very pleasant thoughts.

This morning however, his birthday morning, everything was wrong. He was still red and confused from the

Policeman's rudeness. He removed the cover from his machine, placed it in the lower right-hand drawer, pulled up his cuffs, eased his coat and looked over to smile good morning to Miss Sweeney. She wasn't there.

He guessed at once that she was in one of the inner offices taking dictation and he was right, for soon she emerged from Mr. Twitch's office looking extremely angry, slammed her notebook on her desk and began hammering furiously at her typewriter without even glancing in Mr. Wilmer's direction.

"Oh well," he sighed, "I might have known it— everything's wrong this morning." He did not have to wonder why Miss Sweeney was mad; everyone who had any dealings with Mr. Twitch always came away angry.

Mr. A. Wellington Twitch was the Office Manager and was a thoroughly unpleasant creature. He wasn't much older than Mr. Wilmer, but he *looked* much older, for he was slightly bald and was becoming stout, a fact which he tried to conceal by always wearing tightly buttoned double-breasted coats. His neckties always matched his socks and the neatly pressed handkerchief which peeped from his breast pocket always matched the necktie. This handkerchief was only for show; the one he really used was carried in his trousers-pocket and was generally damp and not too clean, for Mr. Twitch usually had a cold in the head.

His full name was Arthur Wellington Twitch and it is

conceivable, though not likely, that when he was young his mother called him Artie or his playmates called him "Art," but it seemed impossible now that he could have ever been called anything so affectionate. It seemed still more impossible that he could ever have had any playmates.

William Wilmer was still thinking about what an unhappy morning it had been when he became aware that Mr. Twitch was standing beside his desk. He was twisting his little black mustache, a sure sign that he was preparing to be particularly nasty, and speaking in a loud voice so that everyone around could hear.

"Well, Wilmer," he was saying, "daydreaming again, I see. It's really a shame that our little duties here should interfere with your slumbers. Perhaps they will not—very much longer. Three mistakes this morning—three: two additions and one subtraction and in the amount of three dollars, eighty-seven cents."

Mr. Wilmer, hot and confused, tried to stammer something about being sorry, but Mr. Twitch was enjoying himself now and went on in a louder and more sneering tone.

"Of course, to a man of your financial standing the sum of three dollars, eighty-seven cents is practically nothing, a mere bagatelle, as it were, but I can assure you that the Safe, Sane and Colossal Insurance Company, Incorporated, does not share your views. Nor does

the Safe, Sane and Colossal Company appreciate your
innovations in the science of addition and subtraction;
and what's more they're not going to put up with it.
Now watch your step, my lad. One more mistake like
this—just one—and you'll be out in the street. And I
can tell you, jobs don't grow on trees these days."

As he strutted off one or two of the clerks tittered,
but Miss Sweeney did not. She looked more angry than
ever and it was some consolation to William Wilmer to
see her nose wrinkle with distaste and the small tip of a
very pink tongue protrude slightly at the retreating back
of A. Wellington Twitch.

She gave Mr. Wilmer a sweet and sympathetic smile,
but he was too miserable now to be cheered by anything. It certainly was being a happy birthday! All he
could do was to keep punching at the keys of his machine and wait for the noontime buzzer to buzz. He
made several mistakes, but didn't know and didn't care.

This morning, it being Saturday, the office closed at
noon. At 11:57 the office boys went up and down the
aisles placing small envelopes on all the desks. William
Wilmer put his in his pocket without even opening it. It
was his weekly wage and he knew that it contained
exactly $34.86, less Social Security, bond payments,
Withholding Tax and so on.

As he emerged from the S. S. & C. Building he noticed that it was much warmer. Spring had really ar-

rived and this made him feel even more depressed. He didn't care much for Saturday afternoons at any time, but in spring and summer he liked them even less. Everyone was always hurrying toward the stations and the ferries and the bus terminals. They were laden with bags, picnic baskets, tennis rackets, golf clubs, bathing suits and Kodaks. He knew they were going to the beaches or to the country for week ends, but he didn't know anyone who would invite him to the country for a week end and he didn't care much for the beaches, he always got pushed around so much—besides, he sunburned very easily.

So he usually went to a movie on Saturday afternoon and to another one Saturday evening. Sundays were different, they were all right. Because then there were the Sunday papers to read and William Wilmer read every one of them from beginning to end. He read the news and the editorials, the scientific articles and the book reviews. He read the real estate advertisements, the Garden Section, the society notes and even the recipes and the funnies. But what he enjoyed most of all were the Vacation Travel Sections; he read every word of those. He read about cruises to the Caribbean and Nova Scotia and Labrador and Alaska. And about the Grand Canyon and Yellowstone Park, where you could feed the bears; about California and Florida. He liked to picture himself clad in immaculate white linens, stretched in a deck chair, while the ship plowed gently through soft tropical seas and the Southern Cross glowed warmly above the horizon.

Somehow in these imaginings that redheaded Miss Sweeney was always there too. He could picture just how well she would wear Southern resort clothes (he even picked out several outfits for her from the better advertisements) and how her coppery hair would seem even more burnished under a Southern sun and how her very short nose would wrinkle even more fascinatingly as she gazed with delight on the beauties of strange far places. Yes, Sundays were all right.

And then Sunday afternoons he always went over to the Zoo and looked at the animals. He didn't know much about animals, but he liked them. They were so powerful and lithe, yet so resigned to being shut up in cages. Somehow he felt a great kinship with them, for after all, his life in the Safe, Sane and Colossal Insurance Company office was pretty much the same as theirs. Only *they* didn't have any Mr. A. Wellington Twitch to boss them around. He was sure that none of the Zoo's keepers would ever dare be as mean as Mr. Twitch—some tiger or puma would have his leg off in a minute.

What with the spring and the warmth and the unpleasant events of the morning Mr. Wilmer was completely upset and out of sorts. Suddenly, with reckless self-abandon, he decided, "I think I'll go to the Zoo this afternoon instead of tomorrow." It was quite a grave change from the routine of eleven years of established habit, but he felt really desperate. Perhaps the quiet companionship of the animals would help restore his nerves, so without giving himself time to change his mind he hastily boarded a bus and went up to the Zoo.

There were fewer people about than he had expected. The sudden warm weather had made the animal houses seem unbearably stuffy and most people were sprawled on the lawns or messing around on the ponds. William Wilmer wandered through the Large Mammal House and paused in front of his favorite cage. The sign on it said AFRICAN LION (*Felis leo*)—and another sign said TOBY. Toby was Mr. Wilmer's favorite, for of all the animals he seemed the handsomest and most resigned. All day he lay with his proud yellow eyes staring fixedly into space, contemptuous alike of old ladies' poking umbrellas or children's tossed candies.

Today, however, he was restless. He paced and tossed and shook his head. He flopped down and stretched his legs, clawed at the floor and rose and paced again.

Mr. Wilmer hadn't noticed. He was still too upset to notice anything much. He kept seeing the Policeman's angry red face, he remembered the sticky Peppermint

Patooties clasped in his hand. He could see Mr. Twitch twisting his little black mustache and hear his sarcastic, rasping voice.

He remembered, too, that other voice, that small far-away one that he had heard in the street when there was no one there but the Policeman and his horse. It was queer, that was; he couldn't imagine what it could have been.

And then he suddenly heard it again! It was the same voice or one very much like it, small and far away, but perfectly clear and distinct. It was saying, "Well, what have *you* got to be grumbling about?"

William Wilmer looked around to see who was talking, but for once, the Lion House was completely empty of people. There was no one at all, except himself and one Keeper, who was way down at the other end, sweeping and whistling softly; it couldn't be he. Astonished, he looked all around again and then noticed Toby's yellow eyes fixed intently on his face. At last it began to dawn on him that it was Toby speaking—speaking to him, and rather irritably. The great lips scarcely moved, the voice seemed to come from somewhere way inside. It seemed very small for a lion, but perfectly clear.

"Well," said Toby, "I asked, 'What have *you* to be grumbling about?'"

Mr. Wilmer didn't know quite how to answer. He

knew Toby could not understand him if he just spoke in his ordinary voice. It ought to be that small faraway sound; far away and small, but clear and distinct. He tried very hard, he did funny little things with the muscles of his throat and suddenly it came! It came from somewhere way down deep, he didn't have to do anything with his lips or tongue, it just came out, small and far away, very much like Toby's or the Policeman's horse's, but a little thinner.

"Why I wasn't—er—grumbling—exactly," said William Wilmer with his new voice. "I was just sort of thinking and talking to myself, I guess. You see, it's been a very upsetting day. There was that unpleasant Policeman and Mr. Twitch—it was mostly Twitch I think that got me worked up—"

"Twitch," snorted Toby, "Twitch—what's a twitch to bother anybody? Young man, did you ever have a *twinge?*" He hitched himself closer to the bars. "Did you ever have a *pain?* A searing, blinding, red-hot spasm burning through your jaw and down the side of your neck like a bolt of slow lightning?" He hitched himself still closer. "Young man, did you ever have a TOOTH-ACHE?"

"Oh, yes indeed," said William sympathetically. "When I was in High School once I had a dreadful time. It was a wisdom tooth—infected—it was really terrible. I know how you must feel."

"You do *not*," answered Toby. "You can't have the faintest conception." He sniffed tolerantly and opened his mouth wide to show the rows of great glistening fangs. " 'Terrible'!" he snorted. "What would *you* know about terrible, with those tiny little chips of teeth you have? Why this single one of mine, upper right eye-tooth—that's the one that's giving me the agony—why that one tooth has more ivory in it than you have in your whole head, and that much more pain too.

"And the trouble is"—he banged the bars irritably—"the trouble is that these blithering idiots can't find out what's the matter with me."

"Why don't you tell them?" asked Mr. Wilmer. "Why don't you tell them, like you've just told me?"

"Tell them?" snapped Toby. "Don't you think I would if I could? It just happens that you're the first and only human I've seen since I was brought to this God-forsaken, dreary country who could understand Animal or speak Animal, the very first. Now if you would only tell them for me—" A fresh spasm of pain caused him to emit a series of heartrending roars.

Mr. Wilmer, politely waiting for the pain to pass, was suddenly conscious of the Keeper at his side.

"Now then, now then," said the Keeper. "Don't be bothering the animal. It's bad enough he is, let alone, what with something ailing him and nobody knowing what. Four days and nights he's been roaring and bellering and me not able to do anything for him, not even clean the cage, that ugly-tempered he is, and him that's usually a lamb."

"It's a toothache," said Mr. Wilmer. "The upper right eyetooth."

The Keeper regarded him severely. "Toothache is it?" he inquired. "Toothache you say—and in the upper right eyetooth? And just what might *you* be, to be telling *me* about his toothaches and eyeteeth? A mind reader perhaps, or maybe one of them Indian physics or swamis? Here's the Director been up with him two nights, and the State Veterinary, and him with his stethoscopes and X-rays and injections and all, and devil a thing can they find ailing poor Toby—and you to be telling me it's the toothache!"

"I'm sure it is," said Mr. Wilmer. "He just told me so. He said—"

"He *what?*" asked the Keeper slowly.

"He *said* it was the toothache—the upper right eyetooth. You see, we were talking about toothaches and how painful they can be and he said—"

The Keeper grasped Mr. Wilmer kindly, but firmly, by the elbow and started walking him toward the door, talking all the while in a soothing tone.

"Sure and it's a *very* hot day, unseasonable really and the sun real strong for this time in April. You wouldn't have been walking without your hat would you, or maybe have a drop of liquor under your belt, or two perhaps, it being Saturday afternoon and all? We'll just be stepping out into the good fresh air now, quiet-like and not making any disturbances—disturbances disturbs the animals, especially in this spring weather." They were outside now and the Keeper steered Mr. Wilmer toward a shady path. "Right down by the lake there," he said, "there'll be plenty of benches, cool and in the shade—sitting there awhile you'll likely feel better."

He went back toward the Lion House shaking his head. "Too bad," he said. "A nice lad he seemed, quiet and well-behaved. He didn't *look* nuts. It just goes to show—you never can tell."

William Wilmer did sit in the shade for a while and tried to collect his thoughts, but it was rather difficult. It had been a most confusing day and he felt very tired. He decided to go home to Mrs. Keeler's and retire right after dinner, he certainly didn't want to go to any movie. He felt as though he *were* a movie, a sort of one-man two-reel comedy.

Sunday morning Mr. Wilmer woke quite early. The soft breeze stirring his window curtains promised a day still warmer than yesterday, the air even *smelled* springlike.

He decided to walk to the corner and get the Sunday papers before breakfast instead of afterward as he usually did. "My, I certainly am becoming unpredictable," he thought.

As he went down Mrs. Keeler's front steps it was almost like walking into a greenhouse, the morning was so balmy. Down the street two whitewings were flushing the pavement with a fire hose and whenever the stream splashed up from the curbing the early sun struck sparkles and rainbows in the dancing spray. The water ran clear and bubbling down the gutters with little brook-like gurglings.

The same feeling of something impending that had come over him yesterday morning was even stronger today. Certainly, plenty had happened yesterday, mostly unpleasant, but that business of hearing the Policeman's horse and talking with Toby had been very pleasant and most exciting, although quite mystifying. It seemed so long ago he wondered if all those things actually could have happened; it didn't seem possible, he must have imagined everything. Perhaps the Keeper at the Zoo *had* been right, it might have been the heat, or something he had eaten. Yet he could still hear those small, clear voices, he could remember exactly how he had done something queer with the muscles way down in his throat and how, without his even moving his lips or tongue, his own small, clear Animal voice had come out, perfectly distinct and understandable to Toby, although apparently inaudible to anyone else.

There was a milk wagon standing beside the curb. The big, dappled gray horse looked tired, his head hung sleepily. On a sudden impulse Mr. Wilmer decided to try out his new voice. He didn't see the driver anywhere, but he carefully clasped his hands behind his back; no use being called down again for feeding someone's horse.

Then William Wilmer did those strange little things with his throat muscles and the small, clear voice came out just as it had done yesterday. "Good morning," he said politely, "quite warm, isn't it?"

The horse opened one eye, fixing it wearily on Mr. Wilmer, and *his* voice came, much like Toby's but even more like the Policeman's horse's. "Morning," he grunted. "Got the time?"

Mr. Wilmer consulted his watch and announced that it was about 7:45.

"Half an hour more," said the horse, closing his eye again. "The rest of this block—down the Avenue—all the next block—down the Avenue—then back to the stables." He suddenly opened both eyes and stared sorrowfully at Mr. Wilmer. "Ever do any night work, young feller?" Without waiting for a reply, he snorted, "Well, don't!" and closed his eyes again.

The rattling of bottles announced the approach of the driver, and automatically, head hanging and eyes still closed, the old horse clopped along to the next building.

William Wilmer, standing in the deserted street, was swept by a great wave of elation and excitement. It *was* true! He *could* actually talk with animals!

He hurried home with the papers, his mind in a dazed whirl. This accomplishment promised to make life much more interesting; week ends would no longer be boring. . . . He didn't dream *how* interesting life was going to be.

At breakfast Mrs. Keeler inquired: "In early, weren't you? No movie?"

"No," answered Mr. Wilmer, "I was sort of tired, it was quite hot yesterday, and I just didn't feel like it."

Mr. Keeler, helping himself to a third cup of coffee, winked heavily. "Spring," he pronounced. "Ah, spring! In spring a young man's fancy—"

Mrs. Keeler quenched him with a glance. "You're not a young man," she said, "and Heaven knows you're not fancy—and as for spring, there's that bedspring in the third floor front you're to fix today, I'm glad you reminded me of it."

"Yes, my dear," said Mr. Keeler, wiping his walrus mustache with a loud swishing noise. "I was considering that, just as soon as I have glanced at the headlines."

He picked up Mr. Wilmer's Sunday papers. "Ah, here's an interesting item—'Zoo's Prize Lion Suffering from Mysterious Ailment.' "

"Give Mr. Wilmer his own paper," Mrs. Keeler interrupted, "and get going."

Mr. Wilmer glanced at the front page and there, staring out with his patient eyes, was a large photograph of Toby. He began to read the article aloud: "Officials of the Central Zoo have been greatly concerned by the inexplicable illness of Toby, the Zoo's oldest and most prized lion. Dr. Wimpole, State Veterinary, has made several examinations and taken numerous blood tests without any result. X-ray photographs have failed to reveal the seat of the trouble. Carrington Carrington-Carr, Director of the Central Zoo, confesses himself completely baffled. Three eminent specialists, summoned last week from Johns Hopkins, recommended a diet of Vitamins A, E, I, O, U, and sometimes Y, but the patient has shown no improvement. A further consultation of experts will take place this morning—"

"Why, that's silly!" Mr. Wilmer broke off. "It's only a toothache, upper right eyetooth; why, just yesterday he said—"

He became aware that both Mr. and Mrs. Keeler were eying him oddly. "And how," Mrs. Keeler inquired quietly, "and how would *you* know it was toothache—and upper right eyetooth at that—and *who* was it said just what?"

"Why, Toby," he began. "He said—" Then suddenly Mr. Wilmer remembered the Keeper at the Zoo yesterday. He remembered the queer way the Keeper had eyed him as he led him from the Lion House, and now saw that same look pass between Mr. and Mrs. Keeler.

"I—ah—don't remember," he stammered, hurriedly. "Do you know, I think I'll walk over to the Zoo this morning"—and he hastily retreated from the dining room.

Mrs. Keeler was lost in speculation as the front door closed. "Funny," she mused. "No movie last night and he always goes Saturdays, out for the papers before breakfast and he never does that, to the Zoo this morning and he always goes in the afternoon—"

"Spring, my dear," said Mr. Keeler, rummaging for the sporting page. "Spring—birds—flowers—Love, maybe."

"Love . . ." said Mrs. Keeler picking up the coffee pot and balancing it thoughtfully, as a discus thrower weighs his missile. "Spring . . . Spring, my love—and spring fast. Bedspring—third-floor front."

Mr. Keeler sprang.

·   ·   ·

As Mr. Wilmer entered the Park he heard a sound that seemed like distant thunder, but the sky was unusually blue and the sun shone warmly. "Must be building a new subway," he thought. As he neared the Lion House, however, he realized that the sound was the roaring of animals. All the lions and tigers, the leopards, panthers and pumas seemed to be holding forth at a great rate, but one set of roars was much louder and more thunderous than all the others. "Goodness, what a noise," said Mr. Wilmer, as he entered the building. It was empty of people, for the morning was still early.

He went straight to Toby's cage, only to find the bars covered by a large canvas sheet on which was hung a sign, CLOSED FOR REPAIRS. The loudest roars were coming from this cage, and between the roars Mr. Wilmer could hear men's voices and the shuffling of feet.

As he stood there two men came hurrying by. One was the Keeper who had escorted him out the day before, the other was a tall worried-looking man dressed in rough gray tweeds. The Keeper spied Mr. Wilmer, paused, and then suddenly pounced on him with a glad cry.

"This is him," he shouted, above the roaring of the animals. "This is him, Mr. Carrington-Carr, this is the guy!"

The tall man removed an unlighted pipe from his mouth and inquired, "What guy, Gallagher?"

"The one I was after telling you about," cried the Keeper excitedly. "Him that said to me yesterday 'twas the toothache was bothering poor Toby; upper right eyetooth he said, didn't you now?" He shook Mr. Wilmer's arm. "Didn't you say 'twas the toothache?"

"Why yes, I did," answered Mr. Wilmer, slightly dazed by the noise and the Keeper's excitement.

The tall man extended his hand and smiled pleasantly. "My name is Carrington-Carr," he said. "Carrington Carrington-Carr, Director here. Keeper Gallagher has told us a rather odd story of your visit here yesterday and of your truly extraordinary diagnosis of Toby's trouble. Tell me now, just what was it led you to believe that it was toothache?"

Mr. Wilmer hesitated, he didn't want *everyone* to think he was crazy; but this man seemed pleasant and intelligent—perhaps he would understand. "Well—you see," he stammered, "he—er—that is—Toby *said* so. We were just sort of talking about things and he said that he had a terrible toothache, upper right eyetooth, and he said—I'm sorry, but his own words were: 'These blithering idiots can't find out what's the matter with me.'"

Mr. Carrington-Carr flashed a startled glance at the Keeper, but went on quietly. "If Toby possesses this remarkable linguistic ability, which we have certainly never noted, why do you suppose he didn't tell *us* his troubles?"

"Why—er—he said that I was the first person he had met who could understand Animal or talk Animal."

"Have you been aware of this great gift long?" the Director asked.

"No sir, I only discovered it yesterday," Mr. Wilmer answered. "It was a great surprise, I can assure you."

"I don't doubt that," said Mr. Carrington-Carr with a slight smile. "Tell me now, just how *does* one converse with an animal? Let us suppose, for a moment, that I am a lion; would you mind just saying 'Good morning' to me?"

"Certainly not," said William Wilmer. He did the strange little things with his throat muscles and heard his small, faraway, clear voice say, "Good morning, Mr. Carrington-Carr, nice day."

"Well, go ahead," said the Director.

"I have—I did," Mr. Wilmer answered. "I said 'Good morning, Mr. Carrington-Carr.' "

Again the Director exchanged glances with the Keeper. "I didn't hear anything, did you, Gallagher?"

"Devil a word," he answered. "I told you he was nuts."

"Perhaps if you really *were* a lion—" began Mr. Wilmer.

"Don't get fresh with the Director—" interrupted Gallagher, but Mr. Carrington-Carr silenced him.

"Nuts or not," he said, "or voices or no voices, the fact still remains that none of our precious experts had been able to discover what Toby's trouble was until at our consultation last night you mentioned this young man's seemingly fantastic story. As you remember, more in desperation than anything else, we took new X-rays of Toby's teeth, and discovered that the diagnosis was absolutely correct. It *is* toothache, and as far as we can tell, it *is* the upper right eyetooth, although we are not absolutely certain on this latter point.

"Come, let's find out," he ended suddenly and led the way through an office and into a narrow brick passage that ran back of the cages. It was a very narrow passage and they had to pass much too close to the bars for William Wilmer's comfort, for all the animals, excited by Toby's roars, were also roaring and pacing their cages excitedly. In the passage, back of Toby's cage, was a group of young men, many of whom carried cameras while the rest had notebooks. Mr. Wilmer judged they were newspaper reporters.

"Stand aside, boys, and leave the Director get by," shouted Mr. Gallagher; "and mind now, none of your flashlights till you get permission, the poor beast is excited enough as it is."

In the cage were several distinguished-looking gentlemen, most of them in surgeons' white coats. There were two Keepers, armed with heavy iron bars, and a table covered with a white cloth on which was spread an array of shiny surgical instruments. The sight of these made Mr. Wilmer feel somewhat sickish, so he turned his attention to the patient.

Poor Toby looked far from dignified or resigned. He was spread-eagled out on the floor; heavy ropes stretched from his paws to the four corners of the cage. A thick piece of wood was stuck between his jaws and lashed tightly with stout cords, but he managed to keep up a continual roaring and moaning in spite of the gag.

"Gentlemen," said Director Carrington-Carr, raising his hand for attention, "allow me to present Mr.—er—"

"Wilmer," said Mr. Wilmer, "William Wilmer."

"Gentlemen," went on the Director, "Mr. Wilmer is the young man whose uncannily accurate diagnosis enabled us to locate the seat of Toby's trouble. You will, of course, recollect Keeper Gallagher's extraordinary tale at our consultation last evening.

"Mr. Wilmer, it seems, by his own account, was enabled to accomplish this remarkable diagnosis by conversing with Toby in a private form of language with which very few humans are privileged to be conversant. In short, he talked to the lion and the lion told him what the trouble was."

At this a chorus of talk and laughter arose from the newsmen and even the dignified gentlemen in white coats smiled broadly.

"Pipe down, youse," Mr. Gallagher warned the reporters as he toyed with his iron bar, "or out you go."

Mr. Carrington-Carr motioned the scientists closer and continued: "We have not time, at the moment, to go into this remarkable phenomenon, if it is; that can come later. The important thing is that this young man's diagnosis has been, thus far, absolutely correct, as proven by our X-rays. He also says that the trouble is with the upper right eyetooth. Of this we have no proof and to pull the wrong tooth of an animal as valuable as this would be an extremely grave error. I therefore propose to allow Mr. Wilmer to converse quietly with Toby for a few moments and make as certain as is humanly possible that we are doing the right thing. It may help us and it certainly cannot do any harm."

William Wilmer knelt down and put his hand on Toby's feverish paw. He did the peculiar things with his throat muscles and heard his small, faraway voice say, "Well, Toby, they certainly have got you down."

Toby answered, *his* small voice much muffled by the gag. "How han I hawk wiv his ham hick in my mou?"

Mr. Wilmer looked up at the small ring of intent faces. "He says he can't talk well with that stick in his mouth. Could you take it out?"

Mr. Gallagher and another Keeper gingerly untied the lashings and Toby disgustedly spat out the heavy stick. "There, that's *less* bad," he grumbled. *"Now what is it?"*

Mr. Wilmer said, "Toby, these gentlemen have at last found out what your trouble is and they want to relieve it as quickly as possible, only they're not absolutely certain which tooth it is."

"I *told* you," Toby answered irritably. "I told you it was the upper right eyetooth; why didn't you tell *them?"*

"I tried to," apologized Mr. Wilmer, "I *did* try to, but they all thought I was crazy. Perhaps I'd better point it out to them, so there can't be any mistake. This is the one, isn't it?" And he placed his finger on the great gleaming fang. Toby emitted a roar that shook the building and brought down a small snowstorm of flaked paint from the ceiling.

"I guess that's the one all right," said Mr. Wilmer, turning to the Director and the attentive scientists.

They went to work at once. The stick was replaced and well tied. Two white-coated doctors shot huge syringes of anesthetic into Toby's gums; then, while the keepers held his head firmly, another doctor clamped a shiny pair of forceps on the upper right eyetooth. He struggled and wrestled and yanked while Toby's roars made the canvas screen flap as though in a summer wind. Finally, with a great heave and a piercing bellow, the tooth came out, followed by a rush of blood. Other doctors hastily closed in and examined the cavity with flashlights and magnifying glasses.

"He's right!" they chorused excitedly. "That *is* the one—badly ulcerated too!"

The exhausted doctor who had done the pulling advanced with the gory fang still clamped in his forceps. "Here it is, Mr. Wilmer," he cried. "That's the baby, you had it right."

But Mr. Wilmer wasn't there. At the first gush of blood he had quietly fainted and now lay flat on the floor, his head under the instrument table.

When he came to, he was in the Director's office. His hair was wet and his collar sopping, for Keeper Gallagher had helpfully tossed a bucket of water over him. His head was buzzing and his eyes dazzled by the continuous popping of flashlights. His nostrils were filled with the fumes of smelling salts and his ears with the shouts of the reporters and photographers: "Give us a smile now, Bud." "Look over here, attaboy." "What's your address?" "Where do you work?" "How's about a smile?" "When did you learn to talk the lingo?" "Married?" "Got a girl friend?"

William Wilmer answered their questions as well as he could, which wasn't very well, for he still felt dizzy and the flashlights made his head ache.

"How's about a few pictures with the animal?" asked

one of the photographers, so they all trooped back to the cage. The ropes that held poor Toby had been eased so that he could lie more comfortably.

"Do you feel better?" Mr. Wilmer inquired anxiously.

"Ever so much better," replied Toby. "Pain's all gone. Jaw's sore though, probably have to eat mush and trash for a few days. I'm certainly grateful to you though."

"Don't mention it," Mr. Wilmer answered. "Sorry I couldn't have helped you sooner."

They took pictures of Mr. Wilmer sitting with his arm around Toby's neck, of Mr. Wilmer patting Toby, of Mr. Wilmer shaking hands with the Director, with the Keeper and with each of the scientific gentlemen.

"Come on, Daniel," called one of the photographers. "Let's have one with your hand in the lion's mouth." So Mr. Wilmer obligingly posed with his hand in Toby's mouth while Toby smiled pleasantly. However, when they demanded that he pose holding up the tooth, he began to turn green again and the Director called a halt.

They had lunch in the Director's office. It was a large, pleasant room looking out through the trees to the lake and it was a very good lunch too, but Mr. Wilmer didn't get a chance to eat much of it, for the scientists kept plying him with questions. Every time he tried to swallow anything one of them would place a stethoscope against his throat and listen. They listened to his head and his back and his chest, they shined flashlights in his eyes and looked in his ears through little silver funnels.

Each of them wanted William Wilmer to visit him in order to undergo more thorough investigation; and before the luncheon was over he had promised to go to Chicago, Boston, Battle Creek, Washington and Baltimore. He hadn't any idea of just how or when he could go, but the gentlemen were all so pleasant and eager that he couldn't refuse.

After lunch Director Carrington-Carr made a short speech.

"Gentlemen," he said, "we have today witnessed a most remarkable demonstration of something—we do not quite know what. Mr. Wilmer's belief in his ability to converse with animals is, I am sure, completely honest and sincere, and certainly seems to have been borne out by results in the case of Toby. However, as men of science it is, of course, our duty to be skeptical of *anything* new until it has been proved beyond the possibility of a doubt.

"I believe I have thought of a method by which we can test absolutely this gift of Mr. Wilmer's. I have here," and he held up a large ledger, "a complete life history of every animal in the Central Zoo; its age, birthplace, family tree, place of capture, date of arrival here, number of offspring, illnesses, operations and so on. This record is kept in my office safe and its contents are known only to me. It would seem a very simple matter to prove beyond all question this ability of our young friend, if we were to stroll about the grounds and allow him to interview various of the animals. If he can extract from them a few essential details of their private lives and if those details agree with our records, I can see no reason for doubting that he possesses some secret method, hitherto unknown to science, of communicating with the members of the animal kingdom. That is, of course, if Mr. Wilmer is willing to co-operate in this experiment."

"I'd be very glad to," said William Wilmer, struggling with a chocolate éclair, "very glad indeed."

It was quite an imposing group which set forth, all except Mr. Wilmer. His hair was still damp and stringy, his hat had been lost somewhere, and his collar was much the worse for wear. On his left walked Director Carrington-Carr and on his right Keeper Gallagher, carrying the official ledger. Behind them came the scientific gentlemen, in top hats and long coats, flanked by two guards to protect them from the crowd of newsmen and photographers. A great many small boys joined the procession, and several dogs and three nursemaids pushing baby carriages. A balloon seller and a peanut vender with his pushcart brought up the rear.

"We might try Lucy first," said Mr. Carrington-Carr.

"Here she is, right here." Lucy was an Indian elephant. She eyed the group with pleasant interest and extended her trunk for peanuts. Keeper Gallagher fumbled in his pocket for peanuts with one hand while he tried to open the ledger with the other.

"Now, Mr. Wilmer," said the Director, as the scientific gentlemen gathered close and the guards shoved the crowd back, "suppose you just ask Lucy a few questions: date of birth, place of capture, date of arrival here —just a few. Take your time and don't be nervous."

"None of them flashlights now," Mr. Gallagher cautioned.

Mr. Wilmer *was* nervous, though; he couldn't help being. He had never spoken with an elephant before, and Lucy, although not especially large as elephants go, did loom up pretty imposingly.

He cleared his throat, did those funny little things with the muscles and in his small Animal voice said, "Good afternoon Miss Lucy, pleasant day isn't it?"

Lucy dropped Mr. Gallagher's peanuts, cocked up one ear and fixed her small twinkling eye on Mr. Wilmer. "Well, goodness gracious me!" she cried. "It certainly is pleasant to talk to someone; why, this is the first chance I've had since I left Burma, out there of course all the gentlemen know how to talk to us, even the little children do, and if there's one thing I love more than another it's talk. My, my, this *is* a pleasure.

What did you say the name was?"—and extended her trunk.

"Wilmer," he answered, grasping the trunk cordially, "William Wilmer. You see," he went on hastily, for Lucy threatened to start chatting again, "I only discovered yesterday that I could talk with you people or I should have called on you sooner. But these gentlemen, Mr. Carrington-Carr, you're acquainted with him I suppose, and these scientists, don't quite believe I can do it —I can't quite believe it myself—and you could help me very much if you wouldn't mind answering a few questions."

"Not at all," replied Lucy pleasantly. "Delighted, I'm sure."

Mr. Wilmer looked at the Director. "What first?" he asked.

"Age," answered Carrington-Carr.

"Oh dear, I don't think I'd better ask that," Mr. Wilmer hesitated. "You see she's a lady. Perhaps we'd better start with birthplace. Where were you born, Miss Lucy?"

Lucy closed her eyes and recited, "I was born in the jungle of northeast Burma, about twelve miles north of the village of Bding Bdang. The village is not far from the border of Assam."

Mr. Wilmer repeated this information to the Director, who was intently studying the ledger. He looked startled, but merely said, "Go on—date of capture."

"When were you captured, Miss Lucy?" inquired Mr. Wilmer.

"Well, 'captured' is hardly the word," Lucy replied with a sigh, "I was captivated, really. It was an extremely handsome elephant in the herd of one Dhingbat Dhong, a resident of the village. I just sort of wandered in and joined the herd. I was young and inexperienced, of course, scarcely forty-eight at the time. That was back in 1915—spring, naturally."

Mr. Wilmer relayed these facts to the Director, who looked still more startled. "Good Lord!" he murmured. "Go on—date of arrival at Zoo."

Mr. Wilmer was startled too, for glancing over Mr. Gallagher's shoulder he had caught a glimpse of these old entries in the ledger:—

BIRTHPLACE: Jungle of N. E. Burma.
PLACE OF CAPTURE: Bding Bdang.
DATE OF CAPTURE: April, 1915.
OWNER: Dhingbat Dhong.

"When did you arrive here at the Zoo, Miss Lucy?" he inquired.

Again she closed her eyes and thought back. "March

27, 1921, and a horrider day I've never known: rain, sleet and a chill that went through my bones like ice-water. I thought then, 'What a nasty climate this is,' and I've never thought any differently. Don't you think it's a nasty climate, Mr. Wilmer?"

"Indeed I do," he agreed. "Terrible." The next question was "Any offspring?" but he decided to skip that one too; after all, he had been calling her "Miss."

"Have you had any illnesses or operations since being here, Miss Lucy?" he asked instead.

"Nothing but head colds," she replied. "I have those a great deal and you can't imagine how trying they can be with a nose the size of mine—not that it's unduly large, but still, five or six feet of nose is *something* when you have a cold in the head. The only serious thing was an infected toe. It was operated on a year ago last January, the sixteenth, I think. Dr. Wimpole did it, very skillful and a charming gentleman, but quite uneducated; I couldn't understand a word he said."

Mr. Wilmer retailed these details to Director Carrington-Carr, who said in a rather dazed way "Check." He closed the ledger, handed it to Keeper Gallagher, and turning to the scientists announced: "Gentlemen, believe it or not, every answer agrees with our records, absolutely. Shall we proceed?"

Before proceeding, however, the photographers had

to have their inning. They took pictures of Mr. Wilmer shaking hands with Lucy, of Mr. Wilmer with Lucy's trunk around his neck, feeding Lucy a peanut, shaking hands with the Director, shaking hands with Keeper Gallagher, and of all the scientists shaking hands with each other.

Then they proceeded to the Crocodile House and Mr. Wilmer interviewed a crocodile with perfect results: every answer checked exactly with the records in the ledger. During the rest of the afternoon he questioned a camel, a hippopotamus, a wart hog, a boa constrictor, an eagle and an armadillo. As each question was answered correctly Mr. Carrington-Carr checked it off in the ledger, his astonishment growing steadily as in a dazed voice he automatically repeated, "Check . . . Check . . . Check." The amazement of the scientists also increased until they even ceased to argue with one another. Several times Keeper Gallagher was seen to cross himself.

The only upset came when Mr. Wilmer attempted to question a Siberian Bear. He was a great towering fellow and seemed friendly enough and eager to talk, but William Wilmer couldn't understand a word of what he said, although he repeated it several times. Puzzled, he turned to Mr. Carrington-Carr. "I just can't understand him," he said. "He keeps saying something that sounds like '*Ne govoru po Angliski.*' "

"What was that?" one of the scientists asked quickly. William Wilmer repeated it as well as he could.

"Why that is Russian," the scientist explained excitedly. "That is Russian for 'No speak English.'"

"Glory be!" shouted Keeper Gallagher. "Of course it would be. He's only been here a week, come Monday. Just off the boat he is and how could the poor beast be learning to talk American in them few days?"

Director Carrington-Carr slammed the ledger shut and started toward the office. "Come, gentlemen," he said; "I think you will agree that this phenomenon has been proven beyond the shadow of a doubt."

When they were all back in the Director's office and the newsmen had been locked out, Mr. Carrington-Carr began: "Gentlemen, what we have just witnessed seems utterly fantastic, impossible, unbelievable—and yet—it seems to be true. I just do not know *what* to think—"

"*I* think," said William Wilmer weakly, "I'd like to go home."

The Director suddenly noticed that he was quite pale and seemed about to faint again. "Oh, I'm so sorry," he said hastily. "We really have put you through quite an exhausting day." He went to a cupboard and brought Mr. Wilmer a small glass of brandy. "Here, take this, it will do you good."

William Wilmer had never tasted brandy and he

choked and sputtered considerably, but it did make him feel better.

"I'll drive the lad home," volunteered Keeper Gallagher. "I've got the jalopy here and I live only a few blocks above his address." He eyed the glass meaningly. "I've not had too easy a day meself, what with Toby and all."

William Wilmer vaguely remembered shaking hands with the Director and all the scientific gentlemen and being led kindly out to Mr. Gallagher's car. He climbed in and promptly went to sleep.

Later, he remembered being waked up at Mrs. Keeler's house; he remembered more flashlights and Mr. Gallagher's officious voice saying, "Make room there and leave the gentleman get to his bed. It's completely exhausted he is, what with conversing all day with the animals and confounding the scientific world and all."

He remembered hearing, as he wearily climbed the stairs to his room, Mr. Gallagher addressing Mr. and Mrs. Keeler. "Shure ma'am, the miracles I've seen and heard this day have me completely unstrung. A glass of beer maybe, to settle me nerves, and I'll tell you events will have your eyes popping out like hardboiled eggs."

(Note: "Mr. Wilmer's Strange Saturday" is taken from Chapters 1 and 2 of *Mr. Wilmer*.)

Jean Craighead George

THE WOUNDED
WOLF

WOUNDED WOLF climbs Toklat Ridge, a massive spine of rock and ice. As he limps, dawn strikes the ridge and lights it up with sparks and stars. Roko, the wounded wolf, blinks in the ice fire, then stops to rest and watch his pack run the thawing Arctic valley.

They plunge and turn. They fight the mighty caribou that struck young Roko with his hoof and wounded him. He jumped between the beast and Kiglo, leader of the Toklat pack. Young Roko spun and fell. Hooves, paws, and teeth roared over him. And then his pack and the beast were gone.

Gravely injured, Roko pulls himself toward the shelter rock. Weakness overcomes him. He stops. He and his pack are thin and hungry. This is the season of starvation. The winter's harvest has been taken. The produce of spring has not begun.

Young Roko glances down the valley. He droops his head and stiffens his tail to signal to his pack that he is badly hurt. Winds wail. A frigid blast picks up long shawls of snow and drapes them between young Roko and his pack. And so his message is not read.

A raven scouting Toklat Ridge sees Roko's signal. "Kong, kong, kong," he bells—death is coming to the ridge; there will be flesh and bone for all. His voice rolls out across the valley. It penetrates the rocky cracks where the Toklat ravens rest. One by one they hear and spread their wings. They beat their way to Toklat Ridge. They alight upon the snow and walk behind the wounded wolf.

"Kong," they toll with keen excitement, for the raven clan is hungry, too. "Kong, kong"—there will be flesh and bone for all.

Roko snarls and hurries toward the shelter rock. A cloud of snow envelopes him. He limps in blinding whiteness now.

A ghostly presence flits around. "Hahahahahahaha,"

the white fox states—death is coming to the Ridge. Roko smells the fox tagging at his heels.

The cloud whirls off. Two golden eyes look up at Roko. The snowy owl has heard the ravens and joined the deathwatch.

Roko limps along. The ravens walk. The white fox leaps. The snowy owl flies and hops along the rim of Toklat Ridge. Roko stops. Below the ledge out on the flats the musk-ox herd is circling. They form a ring and all face out, a fort of heads and horns and fur that sweeps down to their hooves. Their circle means to Roko that an enemy is present. He squints and smells the wind. It carries scents of thawing ice, broken grass —and earth. The grizzly bear is up! He has awakened from his winter's sleep. A craving need for flesh will drive him.

Roko sees the shelter rock. He strains to reach it. He stumbles. The ravens move in closer. The white fox boldly walks beside him. "Hahaha," he yaps. The snowy owl flies ahead, alights, and waits.

The grizzly hears the eager fox and rises on his flat hind feet. He twists his powerful neck and head. His great paws dangle at his chest. He sees the animal procession and hears the ravens' knell of death. Dropping to all fours, he joins the march up Toklat Ridge.

Roko stops; his breath comes hard. A raven alights upon his back and picks the open wound. Roko snaps.

The raven flies and circles back. The white fox nips at Roko's toes. The snowy owl inches closer. The grizzly bear, still dulled by sleep, stumbles onto Toklat Ridge.

Only yards from the shelter rock, Roko falls.

Instantly the ravens mob him. They scream and peck and stab at his eyes. The white fox leaps upon his wound. The snowy owl sits and waits.

Young Roko struggles to his feet. He bites the ravens. Snaps the fox. And lunges at the stoic owl. He turns and warns the grizzly bear. Then he bursts into a run and falls against the shelter rock. The wounded wolf wedges down between the rock and barren ground. Now protected on three sides, he turns and faces all his foes.

The ravens step a few feet closer. The fox slides toward him on his belly. The snowy owl blinks and waits, and on the ridge rim roars the hungry grizzly bear.

Roko growls.

The sun comes up. Far across the Toklat Valley, Roko hears his pack's "hunt's end" song. The music wails and sobs, wilder than the bleating wind. The hunt song ends. Next comes the roll call. Each member of the Toklat pack barks to say that he is home and well.

"Kiglo here," Roko hears his leader bark. There is a pause. It is young Roko's turn. He cannot lift his head to answer. The pack is silent. The leader starts the count once more. "Kiglo here."—A pause. Roko cannot answer.

The wounded wolf whimpers softly. A mindful raven hears. "Kong, kong, kong," he tolls—this is the end. His booming sounds across the valley. The wolf pack hears the raven's message that something is dying. They know it is Roko, who has not answered roll call.

The hours pass. The wind slams snow on Toklat Ridge. Massive clouds blot out the sun. In their gloom Roko sees the deathwatch move in closer. Suddenly he hears the musk-oxen thundering into their circle. The ice cracks as the grizzly leaves. The ravens burst into the air. The white fox runs. The snowy owl flaps to the top of the shelter rock. And Kiglo rounds the knoll.

In his mouth he carries meat. He drops it close to Roko's head and wags his tail excitedly. Roko licks Kiglo's chin to honor him. Then Kiglo puts his mouth around Roko's nose. This gesture says "I am your leader." And by mouthing Roko, he binds him and all the wolves together.

The wounded wolf wags his tail. Kiglo trots away.

Already Roko's wound feels better. He gulps the food and feels his strength return. He shatters bone, flesh, and gristle and shakes the scraps out on the snow. The hungry ravens swoop upon them. The white fox snatches up a bone. The snowy owl gulps down flesh and fur. And Roko wags his tail and watches.

For days Kiglo brings young Roko food. He gnashes, gorges, and shatters bits upon the snow.

A purple sandpiper winging north sees ravens, owl, and fox. And he drops in upon the feast. The long-tailed jaeger gull flies down and joins the crowd on Toklat Ridge. Roko wags his tail.

One dawn he moves his wounded leg. He stretches it and pulls himself into the sunlight. He walks—he romps. He runs in circles. He leaps and plays with chunks of ice. Suddenly he stops. The "hunt's end" song rings out. Next comes the roll call.

"Kiglo here."

"Roko here," he barks out strongly.

The pack is silent.

"Kiglo here," the leader repeats.

"Roko here."

Across the distance comes the sound of whoops and yipes and barks and howls. They fill the dawn with celebration. And Roko prances down the Ridge.

Elizabeth Coatsworth

BESS AND CROC

A crocodile
Grins in the Nile
Ready to eat you
After a while.

OB MADE UP the rhyme just *as* a rhyme at first, but Bess was such a believing child that it was not long before he enlarged Croc into an especial horror for her benefit.

"His name is Croc," explained Bob as they sat alone

together on the bench at the stern of the steamer, watching the slow brown wake widen and widen till it rippled along the muddy banks, "and he's mine."

"How is he yours?" Bess asked.

"Oh, I found a charm on the walls of one of the temples, and I tried it at the other side of the boat yesterday when Grandma was reading to you about the Flood. Suddenly, up came this big old croc alongside the boat—like a log, you know, but warty. And he kind of grinned at me and said, 'What is your will, O Master?' "

"Ali says there aren't any crocodiles below the cataracts any more," Bess argued uneasily.

Bob smiled.

"Well, you and Ali can believe that if you want to. I'm only telling you what I *saw*. He was about twice as long as Papa, and nearly half of him seemed to be mouth, jammed full of teeth, and he will obey anything I say. He has to. If I told him to come right up here on deck and grab you, he'd do it, like a wink."

"You're telling a story!" cried Bess, but she looked behind her. "I'm going to sit with Mama."

Every day the tales about Croc increased. Often Bess, fascinated like a bird before a snake, asked for the stories herself. When the sun was bright and she could hurry off to the grownups, she only half believed them. It was exciting to sit there with her eyes on the banks of the Nile, listening to some new adventure of Croc's.

"You know he's ever and ever so old," Bob would say. "He was *the* crocodile at Kam Ombos. We haven't come to that temple yet, but they worshiped crocodiles there. He had gold earrings and a necklace of gold and lived in a marble tank, and the priests fed him every morning. But one day he got tired of being a sacred crocodile and slithered out of the sacred tank and started creepy crawly, creepy crawly, creepy crawly for the Nile."

Bob's voice had grown very creepy crawly itself, and Bess broke in: "What did the priests do?"

"Oh, they ran out and brought him wonderful offerings and heaps of the food he liked best, but he went on creepy crawly, creepy crawly—"

"*Please,* don't keep on saying 'creepy crawly,'" Bess begged.

"Oh, all right, then. He went right past them and slithered into the Nile, gold earrings and gold necklace and all. He was still wearing them the other day when I saw him."

"What does Croc do all the time?"

Bob was never at a loss.

"He has wonderful adventures! He was great friends with the sacred cats of Bubastis, and whenever they wanted to cross the Nile to go hunting mice on the other side he took them. The chief cat sat on Croc's head, right between his eyes, and the next to the chief cat sat next, and the next next, and so on. He could take forty cats at a time."

"Weren't they afraid?"

"No," Bob declared. "Not even after the time when the littlest cat told such a funny story that Croc nearly died laughing and shook so that he spilled all the cats off his back, and they were laughing so hard themselves that they nearly got drowned, but they all got ashore, somehow. After that, the chief cat made it a rule that no one should tell funny stories while they were crossing the river."

Another day Bob told about Croc's other friend, the hawk at Edfu.

"See that hawk over the river now? He's probably going to tell Croc a secret. The hawks still tell Croc everything that happens in the air and the cats tell him everything that happens on land, and of course he *knows* everything that happens in the water. So he's the wisest animal that ever lived."

"Then why does he have to obey you?" Bess inquired.

"Because I know the charm," Bob declared and went off whistling.

The darker side of Croc's history was kept for bedtime. After Mama had heard their prayers and kissed them good night and the cabin was dark and the grownup people's voices from the deck came faint and far away, and the water slithered and gurgled against the steamer's sides, and the woodwork gave low creaks and sudden rappings—then, oh, then was the hour of Croc the Horrible.

"Bess," Bob's voice would come like a hiss from the upper berth.

"Yes," poor Bess would answer from the berth below, beginning to tremble.

"Can you hear him?" They always whispered when they talked at night. Everyone seemed to whisper in the dark.

Bess would strain her ears. That sliding sound, that rattle! In a whisper, thin and scared, she would answer, "Yes."

"He's under your berth," Bob's voice would drift down through the darkness. "But I've told him not to bite you. At least if you do as I say. Will you obey me all tomorrow? And give me that green pencil with the eraser?"

"Oh, yes!"

Something enormous and scaly was moving under Bess's berth. She could hear the rub of its heavy body, the clatter of its claws. She drew herself up into a forlorn little bunch against the wall and covered her head with the bedclothes. But well she knew that those great jaws would not be stopped by bedclothes! And through them Bob's voice, raised a little, still reached her.

"Are you listening? You'd better answer when I ask you a question. Did I tell you what Croc eats?"

"No," whimpered Bess.

"I can't hear you. Did you say yes or no?"

"No." This time a little louder.

"Well, he eats one girl a year. Someone fat and tender. Never a boy. He's had his eye on you, but so far my charms have kept him off you. I say those charms every morning and evening."

"Oh, thank you, Bob!" squeaked poor Bess.

One evening after the children had been put to bed, Bess made a frantic request to be allowed to sleep in the upper berth and let Bob have the lower one.

"But why, darling?" Mama asked. "Aren't you comfortable?"

Bess, though a coward, was very honorable. She never tattled. Even now the idea didn't occur to her to tell Mama about Croc.

"I've never slept up there," she whimpered. "I'd like to see what it's like."

Mama considered this, but decided against it.

"You'd fall out," she said. "You're better off where you are."

She leaned over to kiss Bess, and two warm desperate arms closed round her neck, pulling her down. Bess felt Mama's gold watch chain against her cheek, and the crisp white cotton of her shirtwaist. Then Mama pulled herself free with a little laugh.

"Kiss me quick
And let me go
And do not muss
My ruffles so!"

She stood on tiptoe to kiss Bob. The door closed as she went out.

"Bess," Bob began.

"Yes," said Bess.

"It wouldn't have made any difference. Croc would never touch me, because I'm the Master of the Charm. But he could come right out and stand up on his tail and hind legs and lick you out, even out of the top berth, as easy as pie."

"Yes," shuddered Bess.

There was no safe place for her in all the world.

The steamer remained tied up at Luxor for some days. There were wonderful things to be seen there. The temple of Luxor rose just a stone's throw down the river from the steamer's berth, and the passengers strolled off to see it at all times of day. Grandma would bring the Bible there, and she and Bess would find a good block of fallen wall and sit in the midst of the great columns, reading about Vashti or Ruth, King David or King Solomon, and Bess imagined that all temples were exactly like the temple of Luxor. But she liked best the stories about Moses as a little baby in his floating basket, and how he was found by the Egyptian princess among the reeds by the river. Bess knew from the figures on the wall just how Pharaoh's daughter must have looked, all in white, with a gold serpent twisted around her hair and necklaces of blue and gold about her throat. But Grandma went on reading, and the rest of the story got scarier and scarier. Bess couldn't bear the parts about the rod which turned into a serpent, for it made her think of Croc. She would jump up from her seat and walk up and down in front of Grandma in her black silk dress, exclaiming as she walked, "Oh, this is too exciting! This is *too* exciting!"

But even in the most exciting moments, she never walked very far from Grandma, for Bob had told her that Croc was fond of taking his naps in the temple of Luxor.

One evening at dinner there was much talk of the moon. It was to be full that night, and a good many people thought they would walk down to see the temple by moonlight. Papa and Mama said that for once the children might stay up till nine, and as soon as it was dark they started, Bess wearing her scarlet jacket, for it was chilly. Bess walked between Papa and Mama, holding their hands and feeling reasonably safe. Moonlight makes everything look strange. The shadows don't seem to be in the right places and there are too many of them. Besides, Bob had whispered to Bess that Croc intended to come along—"out of sight, of course."

But even Croc's presence, which haunted all her days and nights anyhow, could not keep Bess from being happy in that moonlight. Most of the people from the boat looked about for a little while and then went back to the lighted decks, but Grandma and Papa and Mama and Bob and Bess and Croc lingered. The scars of the centuries faded away in the darkness. Only the beauty remained.

At last Grandma said, "Really, those children ought to be in bed," and Papa drew his watch from his vest pocket and looked at it and said, "Yes, they really ought to be," and Mama said, "I suppose so," and Bob said, "Not just yet," and Bess said, "Do we *have* to go back?" and Croc said nothing, and all six of them slowly began walking toward the lighted steamer.

But they walked slowly, for somewhere a man's voice was singing a tune perhaps as old as the pyramids, and even Bess forgot the present, forgot her fears, forgot Croc, and walked along in a sleepy dream.

At the gangplank they paused to speak to Ali, the dragoman, who was standing there looking at the moon. Mama was asking what the song was about, Bob had already run aboard, and Grandma had followed. But Bess stayed with Papa and Mama. She had forgotten to be afraid. She was looking at the moon. She was listening to the song. And listening, she stepped right off the corner of the gangplank and disappeared into the river below, with a bloodcurdling yell.

She had scarcely time to remember Croc as she took one swallow of Nile water, before she was standing dripping on the bank, fished out by her friend, Ali.

At her scream the passengers came running. Now they stood along the rail, staring at Bess standing shivering in a puddle of moonlit water, her hair in strings.

"Did you slip, darling?" Mama asked anxiously. "What happened?"

The moonlight shone on all those faces which lined the rail.

"No," snuffled Bess bravely. "I just stepped in the wrong place."

"What a funny little girl she is," one face remarked to another. "But I'm glad she wasn't hurt."

Still they didn't go away. They all waited, having nothing better to do, while Mama led Bess through their midst. Wherever she stepped, her shoes squdged out Nile water, and when she stood still for a moment, a new puddle formed about her feet. Her scarlet jacket was a ruin. Her dress clung to her small fat form. She looked ridiculous and she knew it. At that shameful moment Bess would have given everything she had in the world to have sunk right through the deck—yes, even if it had been straight into the waiting jaws of Croc.

(Note: "Bess and Croc" is taken from Chapter 4 of *Bess and the Sphinx*.)

Betsy Byars

THE BLACK FOX

THE FIRST THREE days on the farm were the longest, slowest days of my life. It seemed to me in those days that nothing was moving at all, not air, not time. Even the bees, the biggest fattest bees that I had ever seen, just seemed to hang in the air. The problem, or one of them, was that I was not an enormously adaptable person and I did not fit into new situations well.

I did a lot of just standing around those first days. I would be standing in the kitchen and Aunt Millie would turn around, stirring something, and bump into me and say, "Oh, my goodness! You gave me a scare. I didn't even hear you come in. When *did* you come in?"

"Just a minute ago."

"Well, I didn't hear you. You are so *quiet*."

Or Uncle Fred would come out of the barn wiping his hands on a rag and there I'd be, just standing, and he'd say, "Well, boy, how's it going?"

"Fine, Uncle Fred."

"Good! Good! Don't get in any mischief now."

"I won't."

I spent a lot of time at the pond and walking down the road and back. I spent about an hour one afternoon hitting the end of an old rope swing that was hanging from a tree in the front yard. I made my two models, and then I took some of the spare plastic strips and rigged up a harness, so that the horse was pulling the car, and Aunt Millie got very excited over this bit of real nothing and said it was the cleverest thing she had ever seen.

I wrote a long letter to Petie. I went down to the stream and made boats of twigs and leaves and watched them float out of sight. I looked through about a hundred farm magazines. I weeded Aunt Millie's flowers while she stood over me saying, "Not that, not *that,*

that's a zinnia. Get the chickweed—see? Right here."
And she would snatch it up for me. I had none of the
difficult chores that I had expected, because the farm
was so well run that everything was already planned
without me. In all my life I have never spent longer,
more miserable days, and I had to keep saying, "I'm fine,
just fine," because people were asking how I was all the
time.

The one highlight of my day was to go down to the
mailbox for the mail. This was the only thing I did all
day that was of any use. Then, too, the honking of the
mail truck would give me the feeling that there was a
letter of great importance waiting for me in the box. I
could hardly hurry down the road fast enough. Anyone
watching me from behind would probably have seen
only a cloud of dust, my feet would pound so fast. So far,
the only mail I had received was a post card from my
mom with a picture of the Statue of Liberty on it telling
me how excited and happy she was.

This Thursday morning when I went to the mailbox
there was a letter to me from Petie Burkis and I was
never so glad to see anything in my life. I ripped it open
and completely destroyed the envelope I was in such a
hurry. And I thought that when I was a hundred years
old, sitting in a chair with a rug over my knees, and my
mail was brought in on a silver tray, if there was a letter

from Petie Burkis on that tray, I would snatch it up and rip it open just like this. I could hardly get it unfolded—Petie folds his letters up small—I was so excited.

Dear Tom,

There is nothing much happening here. I went to the playground Saturday after you left, and you know that steep bank by the swings? Well, I fell all the way down that. Here's the story—

BOY FALLS DOWN BANK WHILE GIRL
ONLOOKERS CHEER

Today Petie Burkis fell down the bank at Harley Playground. It is reported that some ill-mannered girls at the park for a picnic cheered and laughed at the sight of the young, demolished boy. The brave youngster left the park unaided.

Not much else happened. Do you get Chiller Theater? There was a real good movie on Saturday night about mushroom men.

Write me a letter,
Petie Burkis

I went in and gave the rest of the mail to Aunt Millie, who said, "Well, let's see what the government's sending us today," and then I got my box of stationery and went outside.

There was a very nice place over the hill by the creek. There were trees so big I couldn't get my arms around them, and soft grass and rocks to sit on. They were planning to let the cows into this field later on, and then it wouldn't be as nice, but now it was the best place on the farm.

Incidentally, anyone interested in butterflies would have gone crazy. There must have been a million in that one field. I had thought about there being a contest —a butterfly contest and hundreds of people would come from all over the country to catch butterflies. I had thought about it so much that I could almost see this real fat lady from Maine running all over the field with about a hundred butterfly nets and a fruit jar under her arm.

Anyway, I sat down and wrote Petie a letter.

Dear Petie,

I do not know whether we get Chiller Theater or not. Since there is no TV set here, it is very difficult to know what we could get if we had one.

My farm chores are feeding the pigs, feeding the chickens, weeding the flowers, getting the mail, things like that. I have a lot of time to myself and I am planning a movie about a planet that collides with Earth, and this planet and Earth become fused together, and the people of Earth are terrified of the planet, because it is very weird-looking and they have heard these terrible moanlike cries coming from the depths of it. That's all so far.

Write me a letter,
Tom

I had just finished writing this letter and was waiting for a minute to see if I would think of anything to add when I looked up and saw the black fox.

I did not believe it for a minute. It was like my eyes were playing a trick or something, because I was just sort of staring across this field, thinking about my letter, and then in the distance, where the grass was very green, I saw a fox leaping over the crest of the field. The grass moved and the fox sprang toward the movement, and then, seeing that it was just the wind that had caused the grass to move, she ran straight for the grove of trees where I was sitting.

It was so great that I wanted it to start over again, like you can turn movie film back and see yourself repeat some fine thing you have done, and I wanted to see the fox leaping over the grass again. In all my life I have never been so excited.

I did not move at all, but I could hear the paper in

my hand shaking, and my heart seemed to have moved up in my body and got stuck in my throat.

The fox came straight toward the grove of trees. She wasn't afraid, and I knew she had not seen me against the tree. I stayed absolutely still even though I felt like jumping up and screaming, "Aunt Millie! Uncle Fred! Come see this. It's a fox, a *fox!*"

Her steps as she crossed the field were lighter and quicker than a cat's. As she came closer I could see that her black fur was tipped with white. It was as if it were midnight and the moon were shining on her fur, frosting it. The wind parted her fur as it changed directions. Suddenly she stopped. She was ten feet away now, and with the changing of the wind she had got my scent. She looked right at me.

I did not move for a moment and neither did she. Her head was cocked to one side, her tail curled up, her front left foot raised. In all my life I never saw anything like that fox standing there with her pale golden eyes on me and this great black fur being blown by the wind.

Suddenly her nose quivered. It was such a slight movement I almost didn't see it, and then her mouth opened and I could see the pink tip of her tongue. She turned. She still was not afraid, but with a bound that was lighter than the wind—it was as if she was being blown away over the field—she was gone.

Still I didn't move. I couldn't. I couldn't believe that I had really seen the fox.

I had seen foxes before in zoos, but I was always in such a great hurry to get on to the good stuff that I was saying stupid things like, "I want to see the go-rilllllllas," and not once had I ever really looked at a fox. Still, I could never remember seeing a black fox, not even in a zoo.

Also, there was a great deal of difference between seeing an animal in the zoo in front of painted fake rocks and trees and seeing one natural and free in the woods. It was like seeing a kite on the floor and then, later, seeing one up in the sky where it was supposed to be, pulling at the wind.

I started to pick up my pencil and write as quickly as I could, "P.S. Today I saw a black fox." But I didn't. This was the most exciting thing that had happened to me, and "P.S. Today I saw a black fox" made it nothing. "So what else is happening?" Petie Burkis would probably write back. I folded my letter, put it in an envelope, and sat there.

I thought about this old newspaper that my dad had had in his desk drawer for years. It was orange and the headline was just one word, very big, the letters about twelve inches high. WAR! And I mean it was awesome to see that word like that, because you knew it was a word that was going to change your whole life, the whole world even. And everytime I would see that newspaper, even though I wasn't even born when it was printed, I couldn't say anything for a minute or two.

Well, this was the way I felt right then about the black fox. I thought about a newspaper with just one word for a headline, very big, very black letters, twelve inches high. FOX! And even that did not show how awesome it had really been to me.

I did not mention to anyone that I had seen the black fox. For one thing I did not want to share it, and then, too, I had never heard that there was such an animal. I had the uneasy feeling that someone would say, "A *black* fox? Boy, you've been dreaming. There's no such thing as a black fox!"

That night, though, after supper I went out onto the porch where Hazeline was sitting waiting for her boy-friend, who was coming to take her for a ride. She was reading a bride magazine and she said to me, "How do you like that dress?"

"It's all right."

"It would look awful on me though," she said. "I am too fat for *everything*."

"I think you're just right. I think people who like to eat are very lucky." I never saw anyone who liked to eat as much as Hazeline, not even Petie Burkis. Every night at the supper table she would say, "This is the *best* cabbage (or sweet corn or beans or beets or whatever we were having) I have ever eaten in my *whole* life."

"Well, I wish I was like you," she said, "and could just pick at my food. You would think that there never was such a thing as a fat bride, because in all this magazine there are only the tiniest skinniest girls you ever saw." She showed them to me.

"Hazeline?"

She was now angrily flipping through the pages of skinny brides, showing them to me one by one. "What?"

"Do you have many wild animals around here?"

"Wild animals?" She paused to turn her mind from the brides. "Law, no, this is practically like the city now. You don't have to worry about wild animals."

"No deer or—foxes, anything like that?"

"Oh, sure, deer, foxes, squirrels, muskrat, the woods are full of *them*. Dad and the boys used to go hunting all the time. I remember they shot a possum one time and it was the ugliest thing you ever saw and it had these tiny baby possums in its pouch. They were so tiny that Daddy had one in a spoon to show me, in a *teaspoon!*" She shuddered and closed her magazine. "I squealed—I just squealed! I thought that possum in that teaspoon was the awfullest thing I ever saw. And Fred Jr. and Bubba used to tease me about that for years. We would be sitting at the table and all of a sudden Fred Jr. would make the awfullest face and say, 'Mama! Hazeline's eating with the *possum* spoon!' That was the only way anybody could ever stop my eating. The *possum* spoon!" She let her magazine drop to the floor beside her chair.

"Hazeline, do you see many . . . foxes in the woods?"

"Why? You want to go hunting?"

"No, no, I just wanted to see an animal or something. I don't want to go hunting ever."

"Well, if you do want to go, you just tell Daddy, because he is never happier than when he's walking through the woods with his gun. He loves it. He could go hunting every day of his life."

"Do people do any trapping or anything around here?"

"No."

"Never?"

"There used to be good money in trapping, I guess, but now they got fur farms and things. Nobody I know does any trapping, unless it's 'cause an animal gets to be a bother, like in the garden or with the chickens."

"Then what do they do?"

"Well, you know that house right on the opposite side of the road where you turn in to our place?"

I said quickly, "Yes."

"Well, it hadn't been but about two weeks ago that

· : 119 : ·

something was stealing that man's chickens. Every night a chicken would be gone, and he knew it was a fox."

"How did he know that?"

"These chickens were taken just before they roosted or real early in the morning, maybe. If a hen's taken from a high perch or something, then it's generally a coon or an owl. If there's some of the chicken left uneaten, then it's generally a weasel or a skunk. But if the chicken's just gone—just carried off whole with maybe a feather or two left behind—then it's a fox."

"Oh."

"Usually a fox won't bother your chickens except when it's got a family of little foxes or something. Then it'll come right on in and take what it wants and not make a noise doing it."

"What did the man do?"

"Mr. Hunter tried going out with his gun but he couldn't get near that fox. Foxes are tricky—that's not something that's just in stories. They really are tricky. So Mr. Hunter got real tired of the whole thing and he went down to the creek and he put a piece of raw chicken out in the middle of the stream on a little island that the fox couldn't reach." She broke off. "Well, at last here comes that boyfriend of mine."

"Yes, but go on about the fox."

"Wait a minute." She waited till her boyfriend got out of the car and then she called, "Well, you were so late getting here that I just went and got me a new boyfriend." She laughed and hooked her arm through mine.

"Well, then," he said, "I reckon I'd just be wasting my time around here." And he turned around and pretended to head back to the car.

"Mikey Galter, you come right back here."

He came back and sat on the porch railing, grinned, tugged at the hem of her skirt, and said, "You look mighty good."

I said, "Go on about the fox, Hazeline."

She laughed and said, "Where was I? Almost losing my boyfriend put that fox right out of my head."

"Mr. Hunter put the raw chicken on the island so the fox couldn't reach it," I prompted.

"Yeah, well, then he put some moss in the stream like a little stepping stone, see? Only underneath the moss was an open trap, and that very night the fox came by and he saw the raw chicken and he put his foot right on that moss and sprung the trap. Bingo!"

"Oh."

"End of fox," she said. "That was about two weeks ago, and then he found the den and went and got a stick of dynamite and blew it up and that was the end of the baby foxes."

"Oh." It was one of those stories that you're sorry afterward that you made somebody tell you.

Mikey said, "My grandaddy was the one who could get foxes. He used to be able to squeak them up."

"What are you talking about?" Hazeline asked.

"There was a place like a hollow, where there were wood mice, and my grandaddy would get down in there and hide and start squeaking. That man sounded more like a mouse than any mouse. He could get a fox in rifle range every time. They just couldn't resist his squeaking."

Hazeline said, real delighted, "I didn't know your grandaddy could do that."

Mikey nodded. "He was in the kitchen one time and he started squeaking and my mom came in and said, real worried, 'There's a mouse somewhere in this kitchen. I hear it!'"

"Your mama?" Hazeline asked.

"She's scared of mice, I'm telling you."

"Not *your* mama?"

"Yes, *my* mama."

They got up an argument about whether his mother was really scared of mice or not, and I said, "I thought foxes were very smart."

"They're smart, all right," Mikey said. "I got the smartest dog in the world and he has yet to catch him a fox. They been fooling him for ten years."

"Henry? Is that who you're calling the smartest dog in the world?" Hazeline said, and then they started arguing about whether Henry was smart or dumb.

"Are we going to sit here and fight all night, or are we going for a ride?" Mikey said finally.

"Let me get my sweater," Hazeline said. She did and then they went down the steps, Hazeline saying, "Next time I see your grandaddy in church I'm going to ask him if he'll squeak like a mouse for me."

I sat there a minute and then Aunt Millie called, "Tom, come in here a minute."

I went in the hall and she was standing back by the bookcase. She said, "Your mother told me how much you like to read and we have just bushels of books right here. You take whatever you want."

She opened the little glass doors so I could see the books and they were all the kind I didn't like. The way I liked to get a book was this:

I would go over to Petie's and he would be sitting on the porch reading. He would be so interested in the book that he wouldn't even look up to see who I was.

"What are you reading, Petie?"

He would lift the book so I could see the title and it would be something like *Mystery of the Deep*.

"Can I read it when you're through?"

He would nod.

"How much more you got?"

Still without missing a word, he would flip the remaining pages.

"Well, hurry up, will you?"

He would nod again, but Petie Burkis had never hurried through a book in his life. So I would wait. And I would wait. And wait. And finally, when I was ready to go out and get the book out of the library myself, then he would come over and give it to me. I couldn't get it open fast enough and I would start reading on my way into the house and the book would start like, "The crack in the earth appeared during the night and when the people of Pittsburgh awoke, it was there, and deep down in the crack the people could see something moving."

That was the way I liked to get a book. I did not like to open a bookcase, especially with someone watching, and know that I had to take one, *had* to.

"This one looks good," I said. It was the kind of book I particularly hated. It was called *The Lamb Who Thought He Was a Cat*. I used to wish people wouldn't write books like that. It would make me feel sad to read about someone who was trying to be something he could never, ever be in his whole life. Just thinking about that lamb worrying because he couldn't climb trees or because he didn't have claws made me feel awful.

"That's a wonderful book," Aunt Millie said. "We

laughed over that thing. I can still remember Bubba sitting in that chair right over there laughing at that book." She looked pleased at my selection.

"I think I'll take it outside," I said.

"Now, listen, when it starts getting dark, you come in. I don't want you to ruin your eyes."

Ruining my eyes was something she did not have to worry about, but adults always seemed to be worrying about the wrong things. One time Petie Burkis's sitter came out and Petie was stuck up in this tree, about to fall, and she said, "Petie, come down out of that wind— you're going to get the earache!" Petie made up a head-line about it—BOY BREAKS TWENTY-SEVEN BONES—AVOIDS EARACHE!

"Now, when it gets dark, come on in."

"Sure."

I went out and sat by the creek on the very rock I had sat on that morning. I did not open the book. I turned it front down on the grass beside me, because I did not even want to see the lamb and the cat on the cover. And I sat there looking across the field, waiting, hoping for some miracle that would bring the black fox leaping over the green, green grass again.

The next four days I spent practically the whole time down by the creek waiting to see the black fox. I am not a good and patient waiter. I like to have things go ahead and happen. I thought one time that if there was some way to turn your life ahead like a clock, then I would probably lose half my life turning it ahead to avoid waiting for things.

On Tuesday I was sitting there as usual, and I don't believe I ever saw anything as green as that field was that day. The sun had turned the grass a sort of golden-green. It was like looking at the grass through sunglasses.

And I thought that if I could discover one thing in my life, I would like to discover a fabulous new color—a brand-new color that no one had ever seen before. Here's how it would be.

I would be digging in my back yard and all of a sudden, while I was just casually digging, I would get this strange exciting feeling that something exceptionally good was about to happen. I would begin to dig faster and faster, my heart pumping in my throat, my hands flashing in the soft black dirt. And suddenly I would stop and put my hands up to my eyes. Because there, in the black earth, would be a ball, a perfectly round mass of this brand-new color.

I would not be able to take it in for a moment, because I wouldn't ever have seen anything but blue and green and all, but gradually my eyes would adjust and I would see—I would be the first person in all the world to see this new color.

I would go into the house and say to my parents, "I have discovered a new color," and my parents would not be particularly interested, because there *is* no such thing as a new color, and they would be expecting me to bring out a piece of paper on which I had mixed a lot of different water colors and made just an odd color, and then slowly I would take my hand from my pocket and hold up the smooth round ball of new color.

That night I would be on the news with my discovery and the announcer would say, "Ladies and Gentlemen, if you know someone who has a color television, go there immediately, because tonight you will see, later in our program, a new color, discovered today by a young boy." And by the time I came on the television, every person in the world would be sitting in front of his set.

The announcer would say, "Now, young man, would you tell the world how you came to discover this new color."

"I was outside digging in the dirt—"

"Where was this dirt?"

"Just in my back yard. And I got a strange feeling—"

"What was this strange feeling like?"

"It was the feeling that I was about to make a new and important discovery."

"I see. Go on."

"And I dug deeper and deeper, and then I looked down into the earth and I saw—*this!*" And I would bring forth the new color, and all around the world a silence would occur. The only silence that had ever fallen upon the whole world at one time. Eskimos would pause with pieces of dried fish halfway to their mouths; Russians who had run in from the cold would stop beating the snow from their arms; fishermen would leave their nets untended. And then, together, all at once, everyone in the world would say, "*Ahhhhhhhhh-hhh.*"

I was so interested in thinking about my discovery that I almost missed seeing the black fox.

There were some old tree stumps in the field that stuck up above the grass. Several times I thought one of these stumps had moved and that the black fox had come at last. I had kept quite still and waited until the stump became, again, a tree stump.

Now suddenly—I was looking in the right direction or I might have missed it—the black fox appeared on the crest of the hill. Gracefully, without hurrying, she moved toward me. There was no wind at all; the air was perfectly still; and Hazeline had told me that on windless days foxes liked to hunt mice. The way they catch them is by watching for the faint movements of the grass. The mice run below the grass in little paths.

The fox crouched low. She did not move. I could see her head above the grass, the sharp pointed ears. She waited, and then slowly, without seeming to move at all, she stretched up, rising tall in the grass. She paused.

Her eyes watched the grass. Suddenly she saw what she was looking for, and she pounced. It was a light, graceful movement, but there was power in her slim black legs, and when she brought her head up, she had a mouse between her jaws.

She turned, her full tail high in the air, and moved toward the woods. I stood up slowly and watched as she trotted away among the trees.

It was impulse more than anything else that made me follow the black fox, and the desire to see where she was going and what she was going to do. I walked quickly across the field to the woods.

I cannot exactly explain my fascination with this fox. It was as if I had just learned a new and exciting game that I wanted to play more than anything else in the world. It was like when Petie Burkis first learned to play Monopoly, and that was all he wanted to do—just play Monopoly. One time he followed me around the yard on his knees, begging me to play with him. And one time he made his sitter play with him and he did everything for her—collected her money, moved her piece, paid her rent. All she did was sit there reading a magazine.

That's the way I felt about this fox. It was a new game. The rules I didn't exactly know yet; all I had so far was a fierce desire to play. My father once said this could be the most important thing in any game.

I slipped through the trees, and the forest was warm and sunlit. All around were large wrinkled boulders. It was as if hundreds of full skirts had been left on the forest floor to dry. There was not a sound anywhere, and I had the feeling I was the only living being in the whole forest.

In English class one time we had to say poems and one girl recited this poem called "Where Are All the Forest Folk?" And when she started speaking, big tears started rolling down her cheeks. There was no noise at first, just big tears dropping down onto her blouse, but when she got to the line "The gay little chipmunk romps no more," she really started sobbing. She could hardly go on she was crying so hard. The teacher said, "Ruth Ann, maybe you'd rather finish later," but Ruth Ann wouldn't sit down, and by the time she got to the last line, which was something like "Oh, where are all the forest folk who were so dear to me?" every girl in the whole room was sobbing. Mrs. Heydon said, "Girls, girls!" and then, "Is there anyone who has a gay poem?" Petie said he was ready with his original composition, entitled "TV Land," but even that didn't help much. You would have thought that the saddest thing those girls would ever know in their lives would be an empty forest.

That, I thought that day, is exactly what I have come upon now. I walked slowly toward a thicket of pines to the right, and just then I heard crows beyond the trees. Hazeline had told me that crows were great thieves. She had once seen a bunch of crows make a fox drop a hen and run off, and I thought perhaps these crows had seen the black fox with her mouse. I charged through the pines and then, to the left, I heard the sharp bark of the fox.

I stood perfectly still, waiting. A butterfly lit on the stone by my foot and flexed its wings. The bark came again. A high, clear bark. I turned and began to run around the pine thicket toward a rocky ravine. The underbrush was thick here, and briars scratched my legs. I ran past the ravine and on through the trees. The fox barked again and I ran even faster.

I don't know how far I went, or in exactly which direction, but I finally stopped by a huge old tree and sat down on a root. There was not a sound anywhere now. I waited. I had had the feeling, all the while I was running, that the black fox had been calling me, leading me somewhere, and now I had lost her.

I turned my head slowly, listening.

(Note: "The Black Fox" is taken from Chapters 5, 6, 7, and 8 of *The Midnight Fox*.)

Charles Boardman Hawes

A TALE OF THE POPLAR

McMASTER WANTED POPLAR, and McLaren cut it. It came down to the dam, and lay so thick in the dead water, where the river spreads to half a mile in breadth, that neither canoe nor *bateau* could pass. So men carried their canoes round the blockade and beached their *bateaux* above; and McLaren stormed because his crews were idle at Number 12. But McMaster was intent on three big lumber deals, and by his orders the "popple" was held indefinitely. It floated on the river day after day until frosts came and puddles froze, and the mud along the edge of the river was crusted on top by the cold. At last McLaren put his crews to work trying to finish a new camp before the first snow.

François Latteau was an artist with the birch-bark horn. For seven years he had worked for McLaren, and each year the same thing had happened. On an October afternoon François would sit down at the summit of the ridge with a great sheet of white bark; he would trim the bark with his keen knife, shape it and bend it, and make it tight with pitch, until he had a long, tapering instrument shaped like a megaphone, with a narrow mouth.

Toward dusk he would go down to the little lake four miles away, where deep woods enclosed the sandy beach and shoals of lily pads; there he would put the bark horn to his lips and utter a long, wailing cry, which began very low, and rose and fell and rose again, until it died away and left all the lake ringing with the echo. As he gave the call, François would wave the end of the horn back and forth and in circles, at first close to the ground, then high in the air, then near the ground again. When he waved the horn an odd quaver came into the call; when the mouth of the horn was near the ground the call was low and muffled; but when the horn was up and pointed into the air it became a full-throated cry that blared into the solitude and silence.

The men said that François Latteau could call a

moose from Mount Katahdin to Suncook Lake by the magic of his voice, and that he inherited the trick from his grandfather, a Penobscot chief.

Very often, as François squatted by the shore of the lake, an answering call would come from valley or ridge or swamp far off among the hills. Then François Latteau would be cautious; hiding under the overhanging brush, he would call, and call again. As the answer came nearer and nearer, now clear as a bugle note, now muffled by intervening ridges, he would change the tone, and occasionally give little grunts and whining sounds that were not unlike the whimper of a hungry dog. At the same time he would stir the water with a stick, and make a noise that was like the splash of a cow feeding in the lily pads. François Latteau was exceptionally clever at this art; he had in his time killed a great many moose.

As the men sat round the camp in the evenings they used to imitate his moose call. François would smile scornfully at their efforts; and afterward, when the men went out to the pond and tried to call moose in earnest, they had no luck.

Barney Osborne seldom tried the moose call; he always sat in silence, listening to the others. Sometimes, however, when the men were telling stories in the evening, he would furtively clasp his hands and hoot so much like an owl that even François Latteau would start in surprise. Barney was a good mimic, and more than once, when François gave the moose call, he had watched every move of the Frenchman, and marked every cadence of the eerie call.

When, with the passing of October, the season for moose came in, François Latteau made a new horn, and the men looked forward to a banquet of moose meat.

The new camp on which they were working was five miles beyond the river, and every day, as they went back and forth to their work by way of the dam, they saw the poplar lying in the dead water.

Early on a Saturday afternoon they started back to camp. François hurried ahead, intent on his moose horn and his gun. Barney Osborne, with a fishing line in his pocket, left the others and set out for a little pond he had discovered, where huge trout would come swirling after the salt pork on his hook. The rest of the men went down the path to the dam, and so across the river to the camp, loafing along in the joy of their week-end freedom.

That day not a trout would bite. Barney soon became discouraged, and started across the ridge through the woods to the river. In his hurry he swerved from the true direction, and instead of striking the river at the dam, came out at the dead water where the floating poplar lay. He started downstream. It was just at sunset, and the logs on the farther shore were tinted with old rose and gold. As he plunged ahead through the brush he came to a great birch tree that towered high above the low spruce and alders. On his left, by the water, was a little beach of coarse sand, against which floated poplar sticks in a thick mass. When Barney looked at the birch and the beach and the few lily pads growing up through the poplar a whimsical idea crept into his mind. He grinned, nodded and drew his knife. In ten minutes he held a long, conical horn, rudely made, but very much like the moose horn of François Latteau.

Barney put the horn to his lips, and moving it gently back and forth, uttered a wavering, long-drawn wail. It echoed from shore to shore, and died away in the evening stillness. Barney tried the call again and again, but no moose came. For twenty minutes he sat by the river, now calling, now waiting in silence. It was nearly dark. He gave a few grunts, holding the end of the horn close to the ground, and stirred a stick in the water, as he had seen François Latteau do; then in disgust he threw the rolled sheet of bark into the river.

As he got up and turned to look for his path his heart gave a great leap of fear; he stood transfixed with amazement and terror. Barney had brought no gun; he had been playing a game, and had not thought of a possible danger. But a beast had come out of the forest like a ghost in the night, as silently as September mist; with savage curiosity it scanned its summoner; red-eyed and sombre, it towered above him. There on the old road, with its mane bristling stiffly, with its antlers flung forward above its widespread forefeet and great tufted chin, stood the king of moose.

Barney raked his mind vainly for an avenue of escape. He could not have climbed the smooth-stemmed birch even if he could have reached it. Behind him lay the river jammed with poplar; beyond that was the camp and safety.

With a swinging shake of its mighty head the beast snorted, plunged forward, and stopped, striking its hoofs deep into the soft ground. Barney took a step toward the river. With a grunt of rage the bull started at him a second time, and Barney leaped from shore. To his ears came a bellow and a splash and many savage grunts. Barney ran with all his speed over the yielding sticks of poplar.

He was an old hand at river driving; he was as sure-footed as a cat, but the poplar had been cut where the growth was young, and the small logs sank under his weight, so that he had not taken a dozen steps before he was running ankle-deep in water. After he had made a hundred feet, his stride lagged; he slumped to his knees, and with the greatest difficulty raised his foot high enough for the next step. He jumped to a trunk large enough to support him, and once more caught his stride; but the shore was far ahead of him and dim in the deepening dusk. His heart was pounding and his lungs ached. Behind him he could hear the baffled moose raging. Barney knew that his one chance of escape lay in unremitting speed, for as surely as he lagged, the poplar would sink beneath him. He pressed doggedly on. As the minutes passed he grew dizzy with the exhausting effort. His foot missed a log, his leg shot hip-deep into the river, and he fell face down.

As he plunged downward he flung himself across the floating sticks, with his arms thrust out before him. The poplars kept him from sinking, but the icy water crept up round his body. He could rest from his terrific sprint, however, and holding his head high, he took in deep breaths of air. He heard no sound from either shore, and looking round, saw that his assailant had departed.

When Barney had recovered strength and breath he decided to go on, and taking hold of two poplars, started to get up. But the instant he shifted his weight to only two sticks they sank beneath him; his arms and knees went under, and his chin bumped hard on the other logs; he drew cold water into his nostrils, and for a moment he sputtered and coughed. The second time he chose his poplars more carefully, and held two in each hand. Priming every muscle for the start, he tried to spring to his feet and get away before the poplars should go under. But he fell again; this time he was entirely submerged. As he rose to the cold evening air he felt blood trickling from his bruised nose. He tried to hitch ahead to the shore little by little, but whenever he pushed one log back beneath him, he lost his balance, and his head went under water; and at best such progress was hopelessly slow.

The chill of the November twilight began to creep into his body; his teeth were chattering and his muscles felt numb. He was soaked from head to foot, and he gradually became aware that his clothes were freezing stiff on his back. A little fringe of ice was creeping out in swiftly forming crystals from the poplar stems. No man could live long in such exposure; in a frenzy of mad fear Barney strove unreasoningly, desperately, to regain his footing on the unstable logs. In his hopeless attempt he almost went entirely under the poplars, and with difficulty scrambled up again to his prostrate position across them.

It was very still on the river. Barney thought of the camp beyond the ridge, where the men were seated after supper, with the cook telling a long story and the "cookee" singing a Scotch song. He thought a little of the Miramichi and a log cabin by a deep spring, and then he began to feel warm and sleepy. The ice was creeping in round him, his clothes were stiffening. He looked at himself as if from a long way off, and he understood that he, the man lying on the river, was in great danger, but that there was a possibility of escape. Yes, he could escape!

With a start Barney woke from his dreaming. He concentrated all his will power and determination to banish the drowsy, comfortable, far-away feeling that made him think that it was time to sleep. Little by little he fought it off, biting his lips and splashing water into his face. When he had gained control of himself he went slowly to work.

He drew many poplars together, side by side, crawling partly over them as he pulled and hauled to make them even. Then with great difficulty he drew more poplars from the water and laid them across the others at right angles. Parallel with the first tier he laid yet another tier. The piled poplars stood inches up from the water. Another layer and another he laid, rolling them carefully together in even crisscross, and taking advantage of every knot, notch and branch to hold them together, for he had no rope to tie them. The raft stood a foot above the water. He was so very numb that he could hardly crawl up on the odd craft, but the effort of building it had saved him. As he climbed, very slowly, one poplar rolled off under his knee, and he rested for a minute without breathing. The raft held, and he lay above water. He raised himself to one knee, to one foot; he almost stood erect when suddenly a side of the raft sank inches under water; the logs tipped and tipped, and then in another moment the whole structure spread apart, and the carefully laid logs spilled in confusion.

Barney Osborne had thought that he could not move, that only to stand would take his last effort; but when he felt the raft lurch and go he made a wild leap. His feet struck a log, and he sprang forward in a lumbering, painful run. It was dark. Above him were small, cold stars and a crescent moon. Ahead, the wooded shores spread dim and low. Under him were deep black water and many poplar logs. He ran faster and faster, keeping his balance by instinct. As he stepped from the logs they made sucking, splashing sounds. His blood moved quickly and more quickly, and his feet, his hands, his legs and his arms tingled with fiery pains. His pumping lungs began to ache, but he never stopped; he ran on and on toward that dim shore line. He struggled on until he stumbled off the last poplar, fell into the water, and in despair let himself go down. But his feet touched the river bed; the water was only two feet deep! He floundered to the bank. Never stopping, he found the old tote road along the river, and broke into a slow jog trot that carried him over the ridge to camp.

He staggered into the cookroom with flushed face and pounding heart, and flung himself down by the hot stove; the men stared at him in amazement. Then from the yard came the sound of slow steps. François Latteau entered with his rifle and his moose horn, placed them very deliberately against the wall, and held his hands over the glowing stove covers.

"For two mortal hours have I hollered at that pond, and never a sound did I hear," said François, scowling vindictively. "There ain't no such thing as a moose left in this country."

Barney Osborne, in the corner by the stove, burst into a great roar of laughter. Loud and long he laughed, while the men stood round in dumb amazement.

Lloyd Alexander

THE CAT AND THE GOLDEN EGG

QUICKSET, A SILVER-gray cat, lived with Dame Agnes, a poor widow. Not only was he a cheerful companion, but clever at helping the old woman make ends meet. If the chimney smoked, he tied a bundle of twigs to his tail, climbed up the flue, and cleaned it with all the skill of the town sweep. He sharpened the old woman's knives and scissors, and mended her pots and pans neatly as any tinker. Did Dame Agnes knit, he held the skein of yarn; did she spin, he turned the spinning wheel.

Now, one morning Dame Agnes woke up with a bone-cracking rheumatism. Her joints creaked, her back ached, and her knees were so stiff she could no way get out of bed.

"My poor Quickset," she moaned, "today you and I must both go hungry."

At first, Quickset thought Dame Agnes meant it was the rheumatism that kept her from cooking breakfast, so he answered:

"Go hungry? No, indeed. You stay comfortable; I'll make us a little broiled sausage and soft boiled egg, and brew a pot of tea for you. Then I'll sit on your lap to warm you, and soon you'll be good as new."

Before Dame Agnes could say another word, he hurried to the pantry. But, opening the cupboard, he saw only bare shelves: not so much as a crust of bread or crumb of cheese; not even a dry bone or bacon rind.

"Mice!" he cried. "Eaten every scrap! They're out of hand, I've been too easy on them. I'll settle accounts with those fellows later. But now, mistress, I had best go to Master Grubble's market and buy what we need."

Dame Agnes thereupon burst into tears. "Oh, Quickset, it isn't mice, it's money. I have no more. Not a penny left for food or fuel."

"Why, mistress, you should have said something about that before now," replied Quickset. "I never would have let you come to such a state. No matter, I'll think of a way to fill your purse again. Meantime, I'll have Master Grubble give us our groceries on credit."

"Grubble? Give credit?" Dame Agnes exclaimed. "You know the only thing he gives is short weight at high prices. Alas for the days when the town had a dozen tradesmen and more: a baker, a butcher, a green-grocer, and all the others. But they're gone, thanks to Master Grubble. One by one, he's gobbled them up. Schemed and swindled them out of their businesses! And now he's got the whole town under his thumb, for it's deal with Grubble or deal with no one."

"In that case," replied Quickset, "deal with him I will. Or, to put it better, he'll deal with me."

The old woman shook her head. "You'll still need money. And you shall have it, though I must do something I hoped I'd never have to do.

"Go to the linen chest," Dame Agnes went on. "At the bottom, under the good pillowslips, there's an old wool stocking. Fetch it out and bring it to me."

Puzzled, Quickset did as she asked. He found the stocking with a piece of string tied around the toe and carried it to Dame Agnes, who undid the knot, reached in and drew out one small gold coin.

"Mistress, that's more than enough," said Quickset. "Why did you fret so? With this, we can buy all we want."

Instead of being cheered by the gold piece in her hand, Dame Agnes only sighed:

"This is the last of the small savings my dear husband left to me. I've kept it all these years, and promised myself never to spend it."

"Be glad you did keep it," said Quickset, "for now's the time you need it most."

"I didn't put this by for myself," Dame Agnes replied. "It was for you. I meant to leave it to you in my will. It was to be your legacy, a little something until you found another home. But I see I shall have to spend it. Once gone, it's gone, and that's the end of everything."

At this, Dame Agnes began sobbing again. But Quickset reassured her:

"No need for tears. I'll see to this matter. Only let me have that gold piece a little while. I'll strike such a bargain with Master Grubble that we'll fill our pantry with meat and drink a-plenty. Indeed, he'll beg me to keep the money and won't ask a penny, that I promise."

"Master Grubble, I fear, will be more than a match even for you," Dame Agnes replied. Nevertheless, she did as Quickset urged, put the coin in a leather purse, and hung it around his neck.

Quickset hurried through town to the market, where he found Master Grubble sitting on a high stool behind the counter. For all that his shelves were loaded with victuals of every kind, with meats, and vegetables, and fruits, Grubble looked as though he had never sampled his own wares. There was more fat on his bacon than on himself. He was lean-shanked and sharp-eyed, his nose narrow as a knife blade. His mouth was pursed and puckered as if he had been sipping vinegar, and his cheeks as mottled as moldy cheese. At sight of Quickset, the storekeeper never so much as climbed down from his stool to wait on his customer, but only made a sour face; and, in a voice equally sour, demanded:

"And what do you want? Half a pound of mouse tails? A sack of catnip? Out! No loitering! I don't cater to the cat trade."

Despite this curdled welcome, Quickset bowed and politely explained that Dame Agnes was ailing and he had come shopping in her stead.

"Sick she must be," snorted Master Grubble, "to send a cat marketing, without even a shopping basket. How do you mean to carry off what you buy? Push it along the street with your nose?"

"Why, sir," Quickset answered, "I thought you might send your shop boy around with the parcels. I'm sure you'll do it gladly when you see the handsome order to be filled. Dame Agnes needs a joint of beef, a shoulder of mutton, five pounds of your best sausage, a dozen of the largest eggs—"

"Not so fast," broke in the storekeeper. "Joints and

shoulders, is it? Sausage and eggs? Is that what you want? Then I'll tell you what I want: cash on the counter, paid in full. Or you, my fine cat, won't have so much as a wart from one of my pickles."

"You'll be paid," Quickset replied, "and very well paid. But now I see your prices, I'm not sure I brought enough money with me."

"So that's your game!" cried Grubble. "Well, go and get enough. I'll do business with you then, and not before."

"It's a weary walk home and back again," said Quickset. "Allow me a minute or two and I'll have money to spare. And, Master Grubble, if you'd be so kind as to lend me an egg."

"Egg?" retorted Grubble. "What's that to do with paying my bill?"

"You'll see," Quickset answered. "I guarantee you'll get all that's owing to you."

Grubble at first refused and again ordered Quickset from the shop. Only when the cat promised to pay double the price of the groceries, as well as an extra fee for the use of the egg, did the storekeeper grudgingly agree.

Taking the egg from Master Grubble, Quickset placed it on the floor, then carefully settled himself on top of it.

"Fool!" cried Grubble. "What are you doing? Get

off my egg! This cat's gone mad, and thinks he's a chicken!"

Quickset said nothing, but laid back his ears and waved his tail, warning Grubble to keep silent. After another moment, Quickset got up and brought the egg to the counter:

"There, Master Grubble, that should be enough."

"What?" shouted the storekeeper. "Idiot cat! You mean to pay me with my own egg?"

"With better than that, as you'll see," answered Quickset. While Grubble fumed, Quickset neatly cracked the shell and poured the contents into a bowl. At this, Grubble ranted all the more:

"Alley rabbit! Smash my egg, will you? I'll rub your nose in it!"

Suddenly Master Grubble's voice choked in his gullet. His eyes popped as he stared into the bowl. There, with the broken egg, lay a gold piece.

Instantly, he snatched it out. "What's this?"

"What does it look like?" returned Quickset.

Grubble squinted at the coin, flung it onto the counter and listened to it ring. He bit it, peered closer, turned it round and round in his fingers, and finally blurted:

"Gold!"

Grubble, in his fit of temper, had never seen Quickset slip the coin from the purse and deftly drop it into the bowl. Awestruck, he gaped at the cat, then lowered his voice to a whisper:

"How did you do that?"

Quickset merely shook his head and shrugged his tail. At last, as the excited storekeeper pressed him for an answer, he winked one eye and calmly replied:

"Now, now, Master Grubble, a cat has trade secrets just as a storekeeper. I don't ask yours, you don't ask mine. If I told you how simple it is, you'd know as much as I do. And if others found out—"

"Tell me!" cried Grubble. "I won't breathe a word to a living soul. My dear cat, listen to me," he hurried on. "You'll have all the victuals you want. For a month! A year! Forever! Here, this very moment, I'll have my boy take a cartload to your mistress. Only teach me to sit on eggs as you did."

"Easily done," said Quickset. "But what about that gold piece?"

"Take it!" cried Grubble, handing the coin to Quickset. "Take it, by all means."

Quickset pretended to think over the bargain, then answered:

"Agreed. But you must do exactly as I tell you."

Grubble nodded and his eyes glittered. "One gold piece from one egg. But what if I used two eggs? Or three, or four, or five?"

"As many as you like," said Quickset. "A basketful, if it suits you."

Without another moment's delay, Grubble called his boy from the storeroom and told him to deliver all that Quickset ordered to the house of Dame Agnes. Then, whimpering with pleasure, he filled his biggest basket with every egg in the store. His nose twitched, his hands trembled, and his usually sallow face turned an eager pink.

"Now," said Quickset, "so you won't be disturbed, take your basket to the top shelf and sit on it there. One thing more, the most important. Until those eggs hatch, don't say a single word. If you have anything to tell me, whatever the reason, you must only cluck like a chicken. Nothing else, mind you. Cackle all you like; speak but once, and the spell is broken."

"What about my customers? Who's to wait on them?" asked Grubble, unwilling to lose business even in exchange for a fortune.

"Never fear," said Quickset. "I'll mind the store."

"What a fine cat you are," purred Grubble. "Noble animal. Intelligent creature."

With that, gleefully chuckling and licking his lips, he clambered to the top shelf, hauling his heavy burden along with him. There he squatted gingerly over the basket, so cramped that he was obliged to draw his knees under his chin and fold his arms as tightly as he could; until indeed he looked much like a skinny, long-beaked chicken hunched on a nest.

Below, Quickset no sooner had taken his place on the stool than Mistress Libbet, the carpenter's wife, stepped through the door.

"Why, Quickset, what are you doing here?" said she. "Have you gone into trade? And can that be Master Grubble on the shelf? I swear he looks as if he's sitting on a basket of eggs."

"Pay him no mind," whispered Quickset. "He fancies himself a hen. An odd notion, but harmless. However, since Master Grubble is busy nesting, I'm tending shop for him. So, Mistress Libbet, how may I serve you?"

"There's so much our little ones need." Mistress Libbet sighed unhappily. "And nothing we can afford to feed them. I was hoping Master Grubble had some scraps or trimmings."

"He has much better," said Quickset, pulling down one of the juiciest hams and slicing away at it with Grubble's carving knife. "Here's a fine bargain today: only a penny a pound."

Hearing this, Master Grubble was about to protest, but caught himself in the nick of time. Instead, he began furiously clucking and squawking:

"Cut-cut-cut! Aw-cut!"

"What's that you say?" Quickset glanced up at the

agitated storekeeper and cupped an ear with his paw. "Cut more? Yes, yes, I understand. The price is still too high? Very well, if you insist: two pounds for a penny."

Too grateful to question such generosity on the part of Grubble, Mistress Libbet flung a penny onto the counter and seized her ham without waiting for Quickset to wrap it. As she hurried from the store, the tailor's wife and the stonecutter's daughter came in; and, a moment later, Dame Gerton, the laundrywoman.

"Welcome, ladies," called Quickset. "Welcome, one and all. Here's fine prime meats, fine fresh vegetables on sale today. At these prices, they won't last long. So, hurry! Step up!"

As the delighted customers pressed eagerly toward the counter, Master Grubble's face changed from sallow to crimson, from crimson to purple. Cackling frantically, he waggled his head and flapped his elbows against his ribs.

"Cut-aw-cut!" he bawled. "Cut-cut-aw! Cuck-cuck! Cock-a-doodle-do!"

Once more, Quickset made a great show of listening carefully:

"Did I hear you a-right, Master Grubble? Give all? Free? What a generous soul you are!"

With that, Quickset began hurling meats, cheese, vegetables, and loaves of sugar into the customers' outstretched baskets. Grubble's face now turned from purple to bilious green. He crowed, clucked, brayed, and bleated until he sounded like a barnyard gone mad.

"Give more?" cried Quickset. "I'm doing my best!"

"Cut-aw!" shouted Grubble and away went a chain of sausages. "Ak-ak-cut-aak!" And away went another joint of beef. At last, he could stand no more:

"Stop! Stop!" he roared. "Wretched cat! You'll drive me out of business!"

Beside himself with fury, Master Grubble forgot his cramped quarters and sprang to his feet. His head struck the ceiling and he tumbled back into the basket of eggs. As he struggled to free himself from the flood of shattered yolks, the shelf cracked beneath him and he went plummeting headlong into a barrel of flour.

"Robber!" stormed Grubble, crawling out and shaking a fist at Quickset. "Swindler! You promised I'd hatch gold from eggs!"

"What's that?" put in the tailor's wife. "Gold from eggs? Master Grubble, you're as foolish as you're greedy."

"But a fine cackler," added the laundrywoman, flapping her arms. "Let's hear it again, your cut-cut-awk!"

"I warned you not to speak a word," Quickset told the storekeeper, who was egg-soaked at one end and floured at the other. "But you did. And so you broke the spell. Why, look at you, Master Grubble. You nearly turned yourself into a dipped pork chop. Have a care. Someone might fry you."

With that, Quickset went home to breakfast.

As for Master Grubble, when word spread that he had been so roundly tricked, and so easily, he became such a laughingstock that he left town and was never seen again. At the urging of the townsfolk, Dame Agnes and Quickset took charge of the market, and ran it well and fairly. All agreed that Quickset was the cleverest cat in the world. And, since Quickset had the same opinion, it was surely true.

Betsy Byars

THE DANCING CAMEL

O N THE HOT, white desert moved a long line of camels. They walked slowly, surely, following one behind the other like a string of beads.

Suddenly the camel at the end of the line gave a graceful hop. She stepped to the side, paused, pointed her toe, turned around, pointed her toe again, bowed, and then followed the other camels.

No one in the caravan noticed what the last camel had done, and the camels moved on as before.

After a while it happened again. The last camel gave two hops, turned to the right, turned to the left, swayed back and forth, clapped her feet together, ended in a graceful bow, and then followed the other camels. No one in the caravan noticed what the last camel had done, and the camels moved on as before.

All across the desert, while the other camels moved slowly and evenly, the last camel, Camilla, was stepping and pointing and bowing and spinning and swaying.

Now it happened that a lone man on a camel was passing the same way. He was known as Abul the Tricky, and he was making his way from the town which could be seen on the horizon. As he sat on his camel, he looked toward the caravan.

The camels moved slowly, surely, following one behind the other. Suddenly at the end of the line Camilla gave a light leap. She crossed her legs, pointed her toes, hopped backward and forward, bowed sedately, then followed the other camels.

No one in the caravan noticed what she had done, and the caravan moved on as before.

But Abul the Tricky had noticed. He passed his hand over his eyes. "Does the sun play tricks on me," he asked, sitting straighter on his camel, "or was that a *dancing* camel?"

He shielded his eyes from the sun and stared through

the waving heat to the last camel. He urged his own camel closer.

"It could not be," he muttered. "Such a thing could not be."

Suddenly, as he watched, the last camel in the line paused. She stamped her right foot, stamped her left foot, tossed her head two times and then spun slowly around, falling finally into a graceful crouch. Then, with another toss of her head, she rose and followed the other camels.

"It is! A dancing camel!" he cried, pressing his camel into a run. "I have got to have her." He threw back his head and laughed in his delight. "Ah, there is no other camel in the world such as this. She will be famous. First she will dance in the market place, then in the Sultan's Palace, then all over the world. I MUST have that camel."

Without pausing, he rode to the front of the caravan and raised one hand in greeting to the leader.

When the leader of the caravan saw Abul the Tricky, he stopped and tapped his camel lightly. The camel knelt so he could dismount.

"I am Abul," said Abul the Tricky with a slight bow. "And you? You are the owner of these camels?"

"That is right," said the leader. "What is it you want?"

"I do not know if you are aware of this," Abul said, stepping closer, "but there is something wrong with the last camel in your caravan."

The caravan leader turned slowly to look at the end of the line where Camilla was spinning with one foot in the air.

"Camilla Camel? There is nothing wrong with her."

"But I saw her! While the other camels walk, she moves this way—she moves that way."

"Oh, yes, she moves this way, that way. She is a dancing camel."

"I should think she would not be a good worker," Abul the Tricky said with his eyes closing slightly.

"No, she is not a worker, but she is a pleasing animal."

"I tell you. I could use a camel such as that. She is no worker, as you agree, but I will take her off your hands."

"What would you do with such a camel?"

Abul shrugged. "Perhaps I would let her dance in the market place. Who knows?"

The caravan leader smiled. He shook his head. "You do not understand. Camilla only dances for her own enjoyment, because she is happy here with the caravan. The hot sands, the warm air, this is why she dances."

Abul the Tricky shook his head impatiently. "Sell her to me."

The caravan leader smiled again. "That is not a bad

camel you have there. Let us trade. I will take your camel. You will take Camilla."

"Agreed," said Abul quickly, and while the little caravan paused there in the desert, the exchange was made.

"Come, Camilla," said Abul. He leaned close and put his hand on her neck. "Let us go to the city. There you will begin your life as a dancer. I will give you everything, EVERYTHING, and you will dance for me. That is fair, eh? You will dance and I will become the richest man in the world. How does that sound, my pretty?"

Camilla Camel looked out over the desert. She waited quietly until Abul was on her back, then she began to move toward the city. Suddenly she stopped. She stooped once, straightened, stooped twice, straightened, stooped a third time, and then straightened quickly and pointed her toes five times.

Abul the Tricky laughed, his teeth gleaming in the sun. "Ah, she is dancing!" he cried. "And she is mine, all mine!"

As Camilla and Abul the Tricky entered the city, two men who were standing in a nearby doorway came forward. One was fat, the other tall. The tall one spoke first. "Ah, it is Abul the Tricky returning to our city. What brings you to our gates again?"

"You will not believe this, my friends, but I am at this very moment riding the treasure of the desert!"

"I see only a camel," said the fat one, squinting in the sun.

"Not *only* a camel, my friend. This splendid beast is a DANCING camel."

The fat man and the tall man looked at each other and laughed. "Last time it was a magic bottle," said the tall one. "We had only to give you a gold piece, rub the bottle, and all our wishes would come true."

The fat man stopped laughing. "I remember," he said darkly. "And before that it was a machine that made gold. Bah! Magic bottles! Gold machines! Dancing camels! You'll not trick us this time, Abul."

"But it is true, my friends. Look on this dainty creature. Is she not fair? Is she not graceful? Can you not recognize a dancing camel when you see one?"

"She looks no different from any other camel," said the tall man.

"Come to the market tonight. You will see her dance. Tell everyone!" He rode on with a wave of his hand. "Tell *everyone*!" He threw back his head and laughed. "Abul has a DANCING CAMEL!"

The word spread quickly throughout the city. Children stopped their play to speak with wide, dark eyes of the dancing camel; men laughed and talked of Camilla Camel over their coffee; women whispered of her behind their veils. Excitement rose. Soon everyone in the city knew that a camel was to dance in the market place that evening.

Only Camilla Camel stood calm in the midst of the bustle and excitement. She looked quietly out over the crowds who came to stare at her. She did not move when Abul placed a scarlet harness with brass bells about her neck. She stepped back only once when the three musicians Abul had hired came and practiced their music in her ear. Her eyes looked always over the wooden roofs of the shops to the long flowing desert beyond.

By evening, everyone in the city was pressing into the market place.

"Make room," Abul shouted. "Make room for everyone. I want everyone to see the dancing camel. There never has been such a thing in all the world. And it is here, here in our little town that she will dance first. Come, everyone!"

He did not need to urge. Everyone wanted to see the dancing camel, and they pressed forward eagerly. Camilla Camel stepped back two steps.

"Quiet, now quiet, please," Abul said with both hands lifted. "In a moment the camel will dance as I have promised, and then these small boys will pass among you and you will put coins in their trays."

A rumble of displeasure came from the crowd. "You said nothing of coins," one man called out.

"Anyone who does not want to see the dancing camel," Abul said, "may now leave the market place."

He waited. No one spoke. No one moved. No one left.

"Ah, how wise you are," Abul said. His teeth gleamed as he smiled. "Someday you will tell your grandchildren that you were in the market place the night Camilla Camel danced."

In the middle of the crowd Camilla Camel moved her feet uneasily, and the brass bells of her harness sounded in the evening air.

"Not yet! Not yet!" cried Abul. "Wait for the music. Now, you musicians, PLAY. Play as you have never played before. And, Camilla Camel, *dance*. DANCE!"

The three musicians lifted their instruments, and the low wail of their music filled the air. So beautifully did they play that some of the people began to sway and pat their hands together. Abul moved in front of Camilla Camel and patted his hands.

"Dance," he said. "Dance, O Beauty of the Desert. Dance! Dance as you danced in the desert. Bow, nod, turn, DANCE!"

Camilla Camel stood quietly in the midst of the crowd. She did not move at all. She did not even look at Abul patting his hands before her. Her eyes looked ever toward the horizon.

"Dance, Camilla, dance." Abul reached down and

touched one of her feet. *"Dance! Don't you remember?"* He tried to lift one of her feet and kick it in the air. "Remember?" He shook her harness so that the bells rang gaily.

Camilla moved her feet closer together and was still.

"Dance, Camilla," said Abul. He began some lively steps of his own to show her what he meant. "See, Camilla? DANCE."

But Camilla looked above him and did not move at all.

"Ah, is this another of your tricks, Abul?" one of the crowd called.

"Yes, where is the dancing camel? We look and look but we see only an ordinary beast."

"Wait, wait," cried Abul. "She will dance. Only give her a moment. Come, Camilla, dance." He turned to the musicians. "Can you play no better? Give her a lively tune, a gay tune. Then she will dance."

The musicians stopped and after a brief conference began such a lively tune that more of the people began to clap and sway in time.

"Now she will dance," Abul said. "Come, Camilla, now you *must* dance. The crowd grows restless. Come, dance."

Camilla Camel did not move. In the midst of the shifting, swaying crowd she stood like an unyielding palm tree.

"Bah! It is only another of Abul's tricks! Let us leave!" one man said in disgust and, turning his back, walked away.

"It is no trick, I tell you. This *is* a dancing camel. Listen, listen, perhaps she is tired—yes, that is the trouble. Tonight she will rest, and tomorrow she will dance. Come tomorrow. Everyone come tomorrow."

The musicians ceased playing, the people began to leave the market place, and the boys who were to pass among the people collecting coins put down their trays.

"Tomorrow morning!" shouted Abul at their backs. "Everyone return in the morning."

But the next morning the market place was only half filled. Abul was not dismayed. "You can be glad you came, my friends," he told the small crowd gathered there. "You can tell the others that you saw Camilla Camel dance in the market place."

"We had better see Camilla dance in the market place, or we leave," said one man.

"She will dance," Abul said. "Come, Camilla, it is time. You have slept on the finest straw, you have eaten the finest food, you wear the loveliest harness. Now you must dance for me." He waved his hand, and the musicians began to play.

"Dance, Camilla, please, dance. Just one simple step," he pleaded.

Camilla shifted her weight once and then stood still.

"Again he tricks us! Come, we waste no more time here." And before Abul could stop them, the people began to depart. Soon Abul and Camilla Camel stood alone.

Abul sat down and bowed his head. "She will not dance. She will not dance," he muttered. "I am ruined. My money is gone. I have nothing left but a camel who will not dance."

Suddenly a shadow fell across Abul's bowed head. He looked up to see the caravan leader standing before him.

"What is wrong, my friend?" he asked Abul.

"What is wrong! Did you not see? I have a dancing camel who will not dance. That is what is wrong."

The caravan leader smiled. "It was not to be. Camilla can not dance here where she is not happy."

"It is easy for you to smile, my friend," said Abul with a frown. "You do not own a stubborn camel who will not dance."

"That is so. I no longer own the camel. And I find, now that I am ready to take my small caravan back across the desert, that I miss Camilla Camel."

"Miss this beast? This stone of the desert?" Suddenly Abul stopped. "You miss this camel?" he asked quietly.

The caravan leader nodded.

Abul got slowly to his feet. His teeth gleamed suddenly in the morning sun. "I tell you," he said. "Of course I want to keep this camel—a dancing camel is a rare animal. But I understand that you want her. I will trade her back to you."

"I will give you your camel in return," said the caravan leader.

Abul hesitated. "But, you see, I have spent much money on this camel. I have bought her this fine harness, food, and straw." He stopped abruptly. "That is a handsome ring you are wearing, my friend."

The caravan leader held up his hand to show a large silver ring set with a white stone.

"An uncle of mine, a man of great wealth, had such a ring," Abul said. "He told me it was a ring of good fortune."

The caravan leader smiled and shook his head. "This is no ring of good fortune," he said. "It is an ordinary ring I bought in the market place."

Abul's eyes gleamed as he bent over the ring. "Give it to me and the camel is yours."

"But this is not a ring of good fortune," the caravan leader protested.

"I must have it," said Abul, stepping forward in his eagerness.

With a shrug the caravan leader twisted the ring from his finger and handed it to Abul. Then he led Camilla away. She went eagerly, her head lifted to catch sight of the small caravan loading just outside the city.

Abul the Tricky barely noticed their departure.

"See what I have!" he cried. "Come, everyone, look."

"What now? How do you trick us this time?" said a man leaning in the doorway of his café.

"No trick, it is no trick. I have a ring of good fortune. Whoever wears this ring has good fortune. See, I have worn the ring only a moment and already I feel my fortune has changed. Who would wear the ring next?"

"I, Abul," said the man. He left the doorway of his shop. "I am in need of good fortune. I have no business. No one comes to drink my coffee."

Abul stepped closer to the man. "For one coin, one small coin," he whispered, "you may wear the ring."

The man drew back at the mention of the coin. "I do not know," he said.

"Very well," said Abul. "I will give another the chance to wear the ring."

"No, no, I will wear the ring. Give it to me." The man took the ring and gave a coin to Abul.

Slowly, one by one, people began to return to the market place. One by one, they entered the café to see the ring of good fortune.

"See," cried Abul in great spirits. "He wears the ring of good fortune only a moment, and already his shop is filled with customers. Come and see, everyone."

"But, Abul," protested the man, "Abul, my shop is

filled, but no one buys my coffee. Abul, hear me, hear me."

Around the café crowded the people. "Abul has a ring of good fortune," they said excitedly.

"Who would wear the ring next?" shouted Abul above the noise.

"I, Abul, I."

"No, I."

Just outside the city, while the people gathered at the café, Camilla Camel was led to the caravan. She took her place at the end of the line. She stood quietly while the caravan leader mounted his camel and rode to the front.

Across the hot, white desert, the long line of camels began to move. They walked slowly, surely, following one behind the other like a string of beads.

Suddenly at the end of the line, Camilla gave a high joyous leap. She pointed her toes, dipped to the right, dipped to the left, touched her toes together, spun around three times, and fell in a graceful kneel. Then she got up and followed the other camels.

No one in the caravan noticed what Camilla had done, and the camels moved on as before.

ABOUT
THE AUTHORS

LLOYD ALEXANDER 1924–

Lloyd Alexander was born in Philadelphia. He attended West Chester State Teachers College, Lafayette College, and the Sorbonne, University of Paris. He married Janine Denni in 1946; they have one child. *The High King,* one of his Prydain series of books, won the Newbery Medal in 1969. *The Black Cauldron,* another in the series, was a Newbery Honor Book. He also won the National Book Award in 1971 for *The Marvelous Misadventures of Sebastian,* and the American Book Award in 1982 for *Westmark.* He was awarded the Regina Medal for his entire body of work in 1986. Other books include *The Wizard in the Tree* (1975) and *The First Two Lives of Lukas-Kasha* (1978). "The Cat and the Golden Egg" is taken from his collection *The Town Cats and Other Tales* (1977), and "The Rascal Crow" is taken from his collection *The Foundling and Other Tales of Prydain* (1973).

BETSY BYARS 1928–

Betsy (Cromer) Byars was born in Charlotte, North Caro-
lina. She received her bachelor's degree from Queen's College in 1950 and married Edward Byars (a professor of engi-
neering) the same year. They have four children. In addition
to winning the Newbery Medal in 1971 for *The Summer of
the Swans*, she also received the American Book Award in
1981 for *The Night Swimmers*, and the Edgar Allan Poe Mystery Writers Award in 1992 for *Wanted, Mud Blossom*. In
1987, she was awarded the Regina Medal for her body of
work. "The Dancing Camel" was published as an illustrated
children's book in 1965, and "The Black Fox" is excerpted
from her novel *The Midnight Fox* (1968).

BEVERLY CLEARY 1916–

Beverly (Bunn) Cleary was born in McMinnville, Oregon.
She graduated from the University of California at Berkeley
and received a degree in librarianship from the University of
Washington in Seattle. She is married to Clarence Cleary;
they have two children. Mrs. Cleary was a children's librar-
ian before becoming a full-time writer in 1950. She is the
author of more than thirty books for young people. Before
winning the Newbery Medal in 1984 for *Dear Mr. Henshaw*,
she wrote two Newbery Honor books, *Ramona and Her Fa-*

ther in 1978 and *Ramona Quimby, Age 8* in 1982. In 1981, she won the American Book Award for *Ramona and Her Mother,* and in 1980 she was awarded the Regina Medal. "Henry and Ribsy Go Fishing" is excerpted from her novel *Henry and Ribsy* (1954).

ELIZABETH COATSWORTH 1893–1986

Elizabeth Coatsworth was born in Buffalo, New York. She graduated from Vassar College and received her M.A. from Columbia University in 1916. In 1929, she married Henry Beston (a writer), and they had two children. A longtime resident of Nobleboro, Maine, she won the Newbery Medal in 1931 for *The Cat Who Went to Heaven.* Her vivid imagination shines through dozens of children's books such as *You Say You Saw a Camel?* (1958), *Lonely Maria* (1960), *The Princess and the Lion* (1963), *Marra's World* (1975), *They Walk in the Night* (1969), and *All-of-a-Sudden Susan* (1974). "Bess and Croc" is excerpted from the novel *Bess and the Sphinx* (1967).

PAUL FLEISCHMAN 1952–

Paul Fleischman was born in Monterey, California. A second-generation children's writer, he attended the University of California at Berkeley and graduated from the University of New Mexico in 1977. In 1978, he married Becky Mojica, a nurse. He is an excellent stylist who utilizes a wide variety of geographical settings. His *Graven Images: Three Stories* was a Newbery Honor Book in 1983, and his collection of insect poems, *Joyful Noise: Poems for Two Voices*, won the Newbery Medal in 1989. "Fireflies" is taken from this latter work.

JEAN CRAIGHEAD GEORGE 1919–

Jean Craighead George was born in Washington, D.C. She received a B.A. from Penn State University and did graduate work at Louisiana State University and the University of Michigan. She has three children. Her *My Side of the Mountain* was named a Newbery Honor Book in 1960, and she won the Newbery Medal in 1973 for *Julie of the Wolves*. Other honors include the Aurianne Award (1958) and the George G. Stone Center for Children's Books award (1969) for *My Side of the Mountain*. Other books include *The Cry of the Crow* (1980), *Coyote in Manhattan* (1968), and *The Summer of the Falcon* (1962). "The Wounded Wolf" was published as an illustrated children's book in 1978.

VIRGINIA HAMILTON 1936–

Virginia Hamilton was born in Yellow Springs, Ohio. She attended Antioch College, Ohio State University, and the New School for Social Research; married Arnold Adoff (an anthologist and poet); and has two children. She won the Newbery Medal in 1975 for *M. C. Higgins, the Great*. She also won three Newbery Honors, in 1972 for *The Planet of Junior Brown*, in 1983 for *Sweet Whispers, Brother Rush*, and in 1989 for *In the Beginning: Creation Stories from Around the World*. She won the Coretta Scott King Award in 1983 for *Sweet Whispers, Brother Rush* and won it again in 1986 for *The People Could Fly: American Black Folktales*. She also won the Edgar Allan Poe Mystery Writers Award in 1969 for *The House of Dies Drear*, and the National Book Award in 1975 for *M. C. Higgins, the Great*. Other books include *The Time-Ago Tales of Jahdu* (1969), *Arilla Sun Down* (1976), and *Zeely* (1967). "He Lion, Bruh Bear, and Bruh Rabbit" is taken from her collection *The People Could Fly: American Black Folktales* (1985).

CHARLES BOARDMAN HAWES 1889–1923

Charles Boardman Hawes was born in Clifton Springs, New York, but was raised and educated in Maine. After graduating from Bowdoin College in 1911, he attended graduate school at Harvard University as a Longfellow fellow, taught, and worked as a freelance writer and editor for *The Youth's Companion* and *Open Road*. He and his wife, Dorothea Cable, had two children.

He was an expert on woodsmanship and seafaring, and his book *The Great Quest* was named a Newbery Honor Book in 1922, the first year the Newbery Medal was awarded. Two years later he became the first American to win the Newbery Medal, for *The Dark Frigate*. Tragically, he died months before the medal was awarded in 1924. "A Tale of the Poplar" first appeared in the December 31, 1914, issue of *The Youth's Companion*, and is reprinted here for the first time.

WILL JAMES 1892–1942

Will(iam) James, whose real name may have been Joseph Ernest Napthali Dufault, was born near Great Falls, Montana (or perhaps in St. Nazaire de Acton, Quebec). Orphaned at four, he was raised by a French Canadian trapper, worked on cattle ranches as a teen, and was educated at the California School of Fine Arts and Yale University School of Fine Art. Both writer and artist, he won the Newbery Medal in 1927 for *Smoky, the Cowhorse*. Other works include *Cowboys North and South* (1924), *Lone Cowboy: My Life Story* (1930), and *Horses I've Known* (1940). "Tom and

Jerry" appears in his *Will James Book of Cowboy Stories* (1935) and is excerpted from an earlier work.

ROBERT LAWSON 1892–1957

Robert Lawson was born in New York City. He attended the New York School of Fine and Applied Arts and married Marie Abrams, an illustrator and writer, in 1922. An artist as well as a writer, he won prizes in both areas, including the Caldecott Medal in 1941 for his *They Were Strong and Good* and the Newbery Medal in 1945 for *Rabbit Hill.* In 1958, his *The Great Wheel* was a Newbery Honor Book. However, he is best known for *Ben and Me* (1939), an illustrated children's book that Disney turned into a featurette cartoon. "Mr. Wilmer's Strange Saturday" is excerpted from his novel *Mr. Wilmer* (1945).

ABOUT
THE EDITORS

MARTIN H. GREENBERG has more than three hundred anthologies to his credit, including several prepared especially for children and young adults. His first trade anthology, *Run to Starlight: Sports Through Science Fiction,* was published by Delacorte Press in 1975. He is a professor of political science and literature at the University of Wisconsin.

Mr. Greenberg lives with his wife and young daughter in Green Bay, Wisconsin.

CHARLES G. WAUGH is a leading authority on science fiction, fantasy, and popular fiction in general. With Martin H. Greenberg and others, he has edited more than one hundred fifty anthologies in a variety of genres, including many for children and young adults. He is a professor of communications and psychology at the University of Maine at Augusta.

Charles Waugh lives with his wife and son in Winthrop, Maine.